SEEK THE STARS

Barbara Cartland

Barbara Cartland Ebooks Ltd

This edition © 2019

ISBNs

9781788672290   EPUB
9781788672306   PAPERBACK

Book design by M-Y Books
m-ybooks.co.uk

THE BARBARA CARTLAND ETERNAL COLLECTION

The Barbara Cartland Eternal Collection is the unique opportunity to collect all five hundred of the timeless beautiful romantic novels written by the world's most celebrated and enduring romantic author.

Named the Eternal Collection because Barbara's inspiring stories of pure love, just the same as love itself, the books will be published on the internet at the rate of four titles per month until all five hundred are available.

The Eternal Collection, classic pure romance available worldwide for all time .

THE LATE DAME BARBARA CARTLAND

Barbara Cartland, who sadly died in May 2000 at the grand age of ninety eight, remains one of the world's most famous romantic novelists. With worldwide sales of over one billion, her outstanding 723 books have been translated into thirty six different languages, to be enjoyed by readers of romance globally.

Writing her first book 'Jigsaw' at the age of 21, Barbara became an immediate bestseller. Building upon this initial success, she wrote continuously throughout her life, producing bestsellers for an astonishing 76 years. In addition to Barbara Cartland's legion of fans in the UK and across Europe, her books have always been immensely popular in the USA. In 1976 she achieved the unprecedented feat of having books at numbers 1 & 2 in the prestigious B. Dalton Bookseller bestsellers list.

Although she is often referred to as the 'Queen of Romance', Barbara Cartland also wrote several historical biographies, six autobiographies and numerous theatrical plays as well as books on life, love, health and cookery. Becoming one of Britain's most popular media personalities and dressed in her trademark pink, Barbara spoke on radio and television about social and political issues, as well as making many public appearances.

In 1991 she became a Dame of the Order of the British Empire for her contribution to literature and her work for humanitarian and charitable causes.

Known for her glamour, style, and vitality Barbara Cartland became a legend in her own lifetime. Best remembered for her wonderful romantic novels and loved by millions of readers worldwide, her books remain treasured for their heroic heroes, plucky heroines and traditional values. But above all, it was Barbara Cartland's overriding belief in the positive power of love to help, heal and improve the quality of life for everyone that made her truly unique.

AUTHOR'S NOTE

Mankind has been entranced, fascinated and inspired by stars since the beginning of Civilisation. The Star of Bethlehem was symbolic of the human search not only for Faith but for Love.

Today nearly every newspaper has columns on the stars, to guide people according to their birth date. Personally I put very little faith in these, as it is very complicated to work out how exactly the time one is born can be interpreted by the stars.

Most of the astrologers, in my opinion, are wrong in what they predict.

For instance Napoleon Bonaparte used astrologers and so did Hitler. They were neither of them told that it would be disastrous to go to Russia and if they did go to leave before the winter started in September.

Napoleon lost half of his Army not to the Russian guns but to the weather.

I can still remember the film that was shown of one hundred and fifty thousand of Hitler's soldiers being taken prisoner, shivering in their summer uniforms, the tanks and guns grounded because the petrol and oil were frozen.

Today the Japanese use the stars continually not just for personal advice but also for their monetary investments on the Tokyo Stock Exchange.

Their astrologers never told them that Pearl Harbour would eventually lead to Hiroshima.

At the same time the fascination of the stars will go on.

We will believe in our hearts that through the stars we will find the perfect Love which, whether they admit it or not, all human beings seek and which only a very few are privileged to find.

CHAPTER ONE
1878

The Earl of Kensall came down the stairs to breakfast at precisely eight o'clock every morning.

His years of training in the Army had made him a very punctual man. He disliked being late himself or being kept waiting by anybody else.

It would have been impossible for anyone looking at him not to be impressed.

Over six feet tall he had square shoulders and was beyond dispute extremely handsome.

Ever since he had been a boy he had been acclaimed for his outstanding good looks and women had fallen into his arms even before he had asked their names.

He was not particularly conceited, but he was well aware of his own importance and determined that his way of life should be one of dignity and success.

As Head of the Family he was looked up to and revered and indeed it was a large family.

The family members turned to him for advice and, when they received it, carried it out to the letter.

His properties, including his large estate in the country, were run in a methodical manner that made him the envy of every other landlord in the County.

The Earl was now nearly thirty, but in many ways he was considerably older than his years would suggest to even a casual observer.

He was extremely intelligent and, when he spoke in the House of Lords, he always held an attentive audience.

The Prime Minister and other leading Statesmen were known to consult him regularly, especially on matters where the National interest was concerned as well as protection of his country from hostile Powers overseas.

The extraordinary thing was that despite his many *affaires de coeur*, he had not yet married.

Naturally his older relations were continually begging him and even nagging him to do so.

"You must realise, Norwin," they urged him repeatedly, "that you need an heir with several younger brothers in reserve to make sure of the succession for your fortune and illustrious title."

The Earl knew that their anxiety rested on the fact that his father had produced only one child, namely himself.

The whole family had been terrified that, while he was abroad serving in the Army, he might have been killed or severely wounded in battle.

That he had survived was in part due to his habitual good luck, which was the envy of all his friends and colleagues.

He was fully aware that the Betting Book at White's Club in St. James's recorded a number of wagers about him, such as whether he would be married before the end of the year or perhaps whether one of the more determined of the ambitious 'Mamas' would capture him to the humiliation of the others.

He had, however, managed deftly to avoid a great many traps that had been set for him over a number of years and so had remained a bachelor.

Older members of the prestigious Jockey Club, who he was closely associated with on every Racecourse, had often as a last resort approached him.

First they would congratulate his Lordship on his horse being first past the Winning Post in a hotly contested race.

Then they would comment on what a magnificent stallion he had recently acquired and would exclaim,

"As I have some excellent mares, it seems such a pity that we don't breed a champion between us!"

"It is certainly an idea," the Earl would murmur.

Then came the inevitable invitation.

"Why not come down to stay for a few days and see what I have to offer, my Lord? Incidentally, my eldest daughter, who is just eighteen, is extremely beautiful."

The Earl would realised that this was yet another trap and so he would of necessity decline the invitation tactfully.

Now he crossed the hall to the breakfast room, which was considerably smaller than the dining room.

Kensall House in Park Lane had been in the family for two generations, while Kensall Park in Hampshire had been in the possession of the Earls of Kensall for nearly four hundred years.

Kensall Park was a magnificent Tudor mansion and it had been altered and expanded extensively by generation after generation of the family

The present Earl's grandfather, who was the sixth in succession, had made it more comfortable and more luxurious than it had ever been before.

The present Earl, however, had added extensively to the Picture Gallery as he had a taste for art that had not been noticeable among his antecedents.

He was thinking now whether he should buy a very fine picture by Holbein, the famous German artist.

It had been offered to him by its owner before being put up for sale at Christie's auction house in

London and it would very certainly be a magnificent addition to his already splendid collection.

However, the Earl had a distinct feeling that, if he bought the picture privately, it might cost him more than if he bid for it in the sale room.

The butler had timed him to the minute.

As his Lordship entered the breakfast room, the butler came in at the other door.

He was carrying in a silver coffeepot which he set down on the silver tray at the top of the table. He then placed carefully beside it the day's editions of *The Times* and *The Morning Post*.

Without speaking the Earl then walked across the room to the sideboard, which was exquisitely carved and gilded and it supported a selection of six silver *entrée* dishes.

There was a different variety of dishes to choose from each morning and they were kept hot by oil wicks burning underneath each one.

As the Earl was ready to help himself, the butler left the room and he was alone.

He raised the lids of each of the *entrée* dishes and finally took a plateful of salmon kedgeree with fresh mushrooms that had been conveyed to London the previous day from Kensall Park.

It gave him a feeling of pleasure to know that he was eating his own home produce rather than what had come from a shop.

He wondered if the salmon had come from the river that flowed through his own land.

Occasionally a salmon was to be found in it and it was, however, more likely to provide him with trout such as he had enjoyed for dinner the previous evening.

Having served himself, he went to his place at the top of the table and sat down.

He then opened his copy of *The Times* at the page that was usually devoted to European affairs by most of the newspapers.

He was particularly interested in the confrontation that was taking place at the moment between France and Germany regarding the price of sheep.

He propped up the newspaper on a silver stand and, as he ate his breakfast, he read a report on what was happening.

He had just finished the salmon kedgeree and was wondering whether he should sample one of the other dishes, when the door opened.

The butler came in and crossed the room to his Master's side.

"What is it, Duncan?" the Earl asked in a slightly irritated tone.

He disliked anybody disturbing or talking to him while he was eating his breakfast.

"Excuse me, my Lord," Duncan replied, "but a lady has just called at the house. She says that it's extremely important that she should see your Lordship immediately."

The Earl raised his eyebrows.

"A lady?" he questioned. "Who is she?"

The butler hesitated for a long moment and then, thinking it would be best to be frank, he replied,

"The lady be heavily veiled, my Lord, but I'm almost certain that it's the Marchioness of Langbourne."

The Earl shifted uneasily in his chair.

Then he said in a low voice as if he was speaking to himself,

"That is impossible!"

The butler hesitated again and then informed his Lordship,

"I've shown the lady into the study, my Lord, and she has asked me twice to inform your Lordship how exceedingly urgent the matter is."

The Earl put his napkin down on the table and rose slowly to his feet.

He did not speak, but was frowning as he walked across the room.

As the butler hurried to open the door for him, he went out into the hall.

He walked down the corridor to the study which was where he habitually sat when he was on his own.

It was a most attractive room with two long French windows opening out onto the spacious and colourful garden at the back of the house.

The walls were covered with books except where two fine portraits of previous Earls hung, one of them painted by Van Dyck.

A footman opened the door and the Earl walked in.

He could now see that Duncan was right.

It was indeed the Marchioness of Langbourne who was waiting to see him.

She had removed what the butler had described as a heavy veil from her face and it was now thrown back over her hat.

An exceptionally beautiful woman, she had not at first been so publicly acclaimed in Society in the same way as she was now.

The 'professional beauties' as they were often dubbed had come into being owing to the enthusiastic attention they received from the Prince of Wales.

The Marchioness had at first escaped his notice and then His Royal Highness had started including her amongst his intimate circle of friends.

The public, informed naturally by the newspapers, hastily appreciated her loveliness and wrote enthusiastic articles about her.

With dark hair and a magnolia skin, quite a number of fashionable artists had begged her to sit for them.

She was also watched for when she drove in state through Hyde Park.

Her husband, the Marquis, had hastily forbidden photographs of her to be published and sold over the counter as were those of other London beauties.

Nevertheless there was a daily clamour at stationers and booksellers for photographs of her.

The Marchioness had been elusive where the Prince of Wales was concerned and this had caused him to pursue her rather more vigorously.

She made him laugh and would flirt coquettishly with him and, because of her witty conversation, she was invariably included in every large party he gave at Marlborough House.

At the same time she managed subtly without offending him to ward off any suggestion that their friendship should be of a more intimate nature.

Then as was perhaps inevitable she met the Earl of Kensall at a smart dinner party hosted by another admirer.

At first glance she was aware that he was exactly the man she had been waiting for with an increasing eagerness.

She was, at the age of twenty-six, at the very height of her beauty and allure and she was quite confident that any man who received an invitation from her dark blue eyes would find her irresistible.

She was the second wife of the Marquis of Langbourne, who was very much older than she was.

In fact he had celebrated his fiftieth birthday a few months before they met and in this he had more than emulated his predecessor.

The Marchioness's first husband had been well over sixty when she married him. Lord Granton wanted an heir and was looking round for an attractive young woman who would give him one.

He was scrutinising the young women in London when quite by chance, when he was at home in his own country house, he met the daughter of a neighbour.

Daphne Wareham had never thought to contract a marriage of such social consequence and she had, of course, heard Lord Granton talked about ever since she was a child.

When his wife died, there had been a great deal of genuine commiseration for him from his friends and family. He was a kindly landlord who contributed generously to many diverse Charities in the County.

Daphne's mother had decided that now she was eighteen, she should appear first at the local Hunt Ball and next at various other County festivities.

Then she would then go to London the following year for the Season.

"I shall be too old, Mama, to be a *debutante*," Daphne protested.

"Nonsense!" Mrs. Wareham replied. "You will simply be a little more sophisticated than the other girls and that will be an advantage for you."

She looked at her daughter before she said,

"Of course, dearest, you may manage to get married before then. There are quite a lot of attractive young men around in the County."

Daphne had agreed with her and she had actually thought that one young man who was to inherit a Baronetcy would suit her admirably.

She had met him out hunting and he would, if he did ask her, be exactly the sort of husband she was hoping for.

They were already quite friendly and yet he had not responded to her rather shy hint that he might like to call on her father and see his horses.

Then, at a garden party given by Lord Granton as Lord Lieutenant, she shone like a star.

Her gown, which had been bought for the occasion was certainly somewhat fanciful for a young girl and her hat was carefully trimmed with small feathers instead of the conventional flowers.

Lord Granton now had no wife to support him as he had enjoyed in previous years and he therefore made more of an effort than he usually did to circulate among his guests.

He greeted Daphne's father, Colonel Wareham, with pleasure because he had known him for a long time.

Then the Colonel said to him,

"I don't think you have met my daughter, my Lord."

Lord Granton had looked at Daphne and then found it impossible to look away.

Most young girls simpered shyly when he addressed them, their eyelashes fluttered and they blushed if he paid them a compliment.

Daphne's eyes sparkled and she managed without any difficulty to hold Lord Granton spellbound by everything she had to say.

During the afternoon he invited Colonel Wareham with his wife and Daphne to dinner the following evening.

By the end of the week he was in love.

It was beyond the Warehams's wildest dreams that their daughter should become Lady Granton and the wife of the Lord Lieutenant of the County.

The disparity in their ages had never even been thought about at any stage let alone commented on.

All anyone could think of was that an ordinary young girl, although her family was an ancient one, was marrying into the Aristocracy.

Lord Granton became as infatuated as if he was a boy of nineteen.

He heaped presents on Daphne and he gave her a horse such as she had never imagined owning.

He also insisted that their marriage should take place as soon as possible.

And so her mother took Daphne to London to buy her trousseau and she was married in the small village Church of Great Downing on Lord Granton's estate.

It was where Daphne had been christened and Lord Granton's first wife was buried.

Showered with rose petals and rice, they set off on their honeymoon as the cheers and good wishes of all their friends in the County echoed in their ears.

To Daphne it was all unreal, but at the same time exhilarating and enchanting.

She was called 'my Lady' and she found herself chatelaine of the huge house that she had looked at with awe ever since she was a small child.

Unfortunately only a few months after their marriage Lord Granton suffered a severe stroke.

For the next two years Daphne sat by his bedside while the doctors came and went, but could do nothing to improve his condition.

When at last Lord Granton died, it was a merciful release for all concerned.

After a long year of mourning Daphne came to London and she was clever enough to persuade a Lady of Quality, who was in strait-laced circumstances, to chaperone her and present her at Court.

She now had plenty of money and could afford to rent a large house in Mayfair.

Expensively dressed she soon began to attract attention.

For six months she dazzled the most sophisticated Society in England before she finally met the Marquis of Langbourne.

Himself recently widowed, he was unhappy, restless and trying to adjust himself to being alone and so he was an easy conquest.

Two months later they were married quietly in a small village Church and now Daphne thought that she had everything she had ever wanted.

There was a huge house in the country, a fine house in London and, although she could hardly believe it, she was by tradition a Lady of the Bedchamber to Queen Victoria herself.

She felt then that she had reached the height of glory such as she had only read about in history books and novels.

For the first year of their marriage she obeyed her husband loyally and did exactly as he wished.

She felt sometimes, as she had with Lord Granton, that he was rather like a father to her and at other times a rather strict schoolmaster.

Then she began to assert herself and she soon had very different ideas of what interested her and what she desired from her life.

She was, however, in no hurry.

The Marquis after a long honeymoon had come back to an endless series of official duties, which occupied him every day when he was in London.

In the country he was also busy with his estates.

Again, as if history was repeating itself, Daphne found herself alone.

She was therefore in a position to choose her own interests, her own amusements and, more importantly, her own friends.

These included men, men whom she entertained and who she danced with and flirted with.

Because she was intelligent, she was very careful not to neglect her husband in any way.

When she finally took her first lover, she was terrified.

She had been concerned about her reputation when she was widowed and now she was frightened in case the Marquis should somehow suspect that she was being unfaithful to him.

The Marquis was often very tired in the evening as he was so busy during the day that, as long as he could see his wife at the end of the dining table, he was quite happy.

He did not realise that she was coming into bloom like a rose and, as a woman rather than a girl, she now required more attention.

She was, moreover, still terrified of doing anything that could damage her name or reputation socially.

Daphne, therefore, had amorous affairs with unimportant young men who remained unnoticed by the gossips.

Only occasionally was the Marquis slightly jealous of her and she would laugh at his suspicions.

"I want only *you* to admire me, my darling," she would then say. "But if other men do so, then that is indeed a compliment to you."

She revelled in becoming 'a public beauty' and she was delighted by the admiration that she evoked and the publicity she received in the newspapers and magazines despite her husband's strictures.

Then she met the Earl.

For the first time in her life Daphne fell in love.

And the Earl of Kensall turned out to be a very much more ardent lover than any man she had known in her life.

He was what she had always craved for, a conqueror and she had secretly despised the men who pleaded for her favours.

The Earl, like 'a Monarch of all he surveyed,' swept her off her feet. He made her surrender to him and took it for granted that he would capture her heart.

He assumed as if by right that she would fall wildly and inescapably in love with him.

He gave her new sensations that she had never known before and, when he left her, she counted the hours until she could see him again.

*

Now when he came into the study where she was waiting for him, she was aware that he was very angry.

He was angry that she should have done anything so indiscreet as to call on him so early in the day.

The Earl closed the door firmly behind him.

Then he said in a sharp voice,

"Daphne! What are you doing here?"

"I had to – come! I had to – see you, Norwin," she cried. "Something terrible – ghastly and devastating – has happened!"

There was no doubt that she was feeling agitated and the Earl thought that to reveal her problems was a mistake.

He had no wish for the servants to talk and he fondly believed that his *affaires de coeur*, and there were a great number of them, were not of interest to anyone in the servants' hall.

He walked slowly towards the Marchioness.

He appeared not to notice that she put out her ungloved hands towards him.

"What has happened?" he demanded. "You know as well as I do that it is a dreadful mistake for you to call on me at this hour."

"I know, I know," Daphne admitted. "But I had to see you and this was the – only way I could do so. Arthur thinks I am in Church."

The Earl looked surprised.

"Arthur?" he repeated. "Are you saying he has returned?"

"He came back – unexpectedly last night," the Marchioness replied. "As you know, I thought he would be away for – another week in Paris, but he – returned because he has had me – watched."

The Earl was startled.

There was silence before he said in a voice that he found hard to recognise as his own,

"Did you say – he has had you *watched?*"

"Y-yes," Daphne answered with a little sob. "He set a detective on me before he went off to

France and, when he received the man's report, he came back without telling anybody what he was doing."

The Earl thought that it was indeed fortunate that he had not visited Daphne last night as he might well have done.

He had attended his Regimental dinner in the Officer's Mess in Whitehall and, when it was over, it was very late and he was tired.

He had been with her the night before and the night before that.

Almost as if she followed his thoughts, Daphne said,

"I was asleep in bed and, of course, alone when Arthur came in. He raged at me, telling me that he had been sent a detective's report of all my movements since he had left England for France."

The Earl drew in his breath.

He knew that, if this was true, he was heavily involved in what could turn out to be an appalling scandal.

Daphne sank down on the sofa and put her hands up to her eyes.

"He read out the report which included all the times when you came to the house and when – you left."

The Earl thought that he had been extremely stupid and he should have realised that there was a man watching him when he left and on some occasions this had been after dawn had broken.

Before he could ask the question, Daphne said in a broken voice,

"Arthur – says he intends to – divorce me!"

"I don't believe it!" the Earl exclaimed.

"He says – that is what he – intends to do – and you know how obstinate he is and how it is – impossible to ever make him – change his mind."

"But you tried to explain – for God's sake, say you tried!" the Earl insisted.

As he spoke, he thought with horror of the position that he was now in.

A suit for divorce, which was very difficult to obtain, would have to go through the House of Lords and every word of the action would be published fully in the newspapers.

What was more, it meant, before the Marquis obtained his divorce, that there would be many months of negotiations between the lawyers.

If the Marquis was successful in the case, as undoubtedly he would be, he, the Earl, as a gentleman, would have to ask Daphne to be his wife.

They would then be expected to go abroad and it would be at least five years before it would be possible for them to return to England.

Even then, while he would be more or less accepted in the men's Society, Daphne would be ostracised for the rest of her life. And no social hostess would ever permit her to cross her threshold.

Then they would be confined to knowing only the 'ragtag and bobtail,' people like themselves, who had caused an unforgivable scandal, or people who were prepared to go anywhere and know anyone for a free drink.

To the Earl it seemed as if he was facing a hell on earth and thought that he would rather die than spend the rest of his life living like that.

"Surely you argued with him?" he quizzed her at length and his voice seemed to come from a long distance away.

"I not only – argued with him," Daphne replied, "I told him it was – not true."

"Did you expect him to believe that?"

"I told him that, when you came to the house it was – not to see me but Sadira."

The Earl stared at her in puzzlement and for a moment he could not think what she meant.

Then he remembered that the Marquis had a daughter by his previous marriage and he had seen her once disappearing down the end of a corridor.

Now that he thought about it, he might have met her at an 'at home' that her stepmother had given in her house. It was early in their acquaintance, when he was still no more than curious about Daphne.

He had no memory now of what the girl had looked like or even the colour of her hair.

"I don't think he is any more likely to believe that," he muttered.

"I told him," Daphne explained, "that – now he had come home you would be calling on him to ask for Sadira's hand – in marriage."

As she said the words, they seemed to tremble on her lips.

"Marry her?" he asserted sharply. "How can I marry a girl I have never spoken to or even met?"

"But you have to – do you not see? *You – have to*!" Daphne almost shouted desperately. "And that is what I have come to – tell you. I don't think Arthur really believes – you are interested – in Sadira, but however much he may threaten me with – a divorce – he will not want a Society – scandal."

"I am sure – " the Earl began.

"Listen, you must listen!" Daphne interrupted him urgently. "He will accept you as his son-in-law simply because you are so important – and that is the – only way we can save – ourselves."

She threw out her hands as she went nervously on,

"You know what Arthur is like – or perhaps you don't. He is above all extremely proud. He cannot bear to think that – you have made a fool of him."

She paused a moment and then continued,

"The only way we can save ourselves is for you to *marry* Sadira and Arthur can save his own face at the – same time."

The Earl stared at Daphne as if he could not believe what she was saying.

He tried to protest that it was quite impossible and that the whole idea was seriously ridiculous, yet he found that the words would not leave his lips.

He could see vaguely, like the light at the end of a very dark tunnel, that this might just possibly be the only way out.

It would be, however, at a cost to himself that was utterly and completely intolerable.

He walked across the room to stand at the window and he gazed out with unseeing eyes at the sunshine that bathed the garden.

'There *must* be some other way," he insisted at last.

"No! There is none! I lay awake the rest of the night after Arthur had raged at me until three o'clock. He called me appalling names, which is something that – he has never done before."

She drew in her breath before she went on,

"You must see, Norwin, that it has been a terrible shock to him. He is old – but he likes to think of himself as young. He has sometimes been a little jealous, but has always believed that I was – absolutely and completely faithful to him."

Without turning round the Earl replied,

"You have been extremely clever in the past. Surely you can do something now?"

"I *have* done something and that is what I came here to tell you," Daphne answered, "When he returned last night, he was determined to throw me out of the house and start divorce proceedings against me and citing you as the co-respondent."

She gave a deep sigh before she went on in a more practical tone,

"I pleaded and begged him – to believe me! I swore on the Bible and on my mother's head that I was telling him the truth."

She looked at him and then carried on,

"I said it was Sadira who you were interested in and it was Sadira you were courting. You stopped at the house telling me how much in love you were with her until the early hours – of the morning."

"And he believed you?" the Earl asked sarcastically.

"He *wants* to believe me, but he will permit himself to be sure that I am unblemished and still faithful to him only if you will do what I have said you will and that is to call on him this morning to ask permission to marry his daughter."

"And if I refuse?" the Earl asked.

"Then, because Arthur is so obstinate, I know that he will start divorce proceedings immediately, as he had threatened to do so fiercely last night."

She rose from the sofa and walked across the room to put her hand on the Earl's arm.

"Please, please, I beg of you – save us both," she pleaded. "I love you and it would be Heaven to be with you always – but you know as well as I do that the humiliation and misery would kill us."

Her fingers tightened on his arm and she asked,

"How can I be – sneered at and – spurned by the women who have – been my friends?"

The Earl did not reply and she battled on,

"How can I be deprived of my position as Lady of the Bedchamber to – Her Majesty the Queen?"

She gave a little sob before she added,

"How could we – go abroad to live in some sleazy French town? We should hate it there – because of what we would be missing in England."

The Earl recognised that this was certainly true.

He was well aware that that it was what a divorce would entail and he was thinking too of how much it would hurt his family.

If the Marquis was proud, so were the Kensalls.

Every Earl had played his part in the magnificent history of England and there had, of course, been some spendthrifts, some incompetent Statesmen and some extremely tiresome characters.

But there had never yet been a Society scandal in the family.

Certainly not to the point where the reigning Earl had been dragged through the Divorce Courts.

Nor, for that matter, had a Kensall been executed in the Tower of London.

To suffer execution at the Tower, the Earl thought, might indeed be preferable to facing the rest of his life with Daphne in exile away from everything he possessed and the life that he enjoyed.

There was a poignant silence until Daphne wailed,

"I must go at once. I managed to get here only by pretending that I wished to attend a Service in the Grosvenor Chapel in South Audley Street. "

"Alone?" the Earl queried.

"No, of course not. My maid came with me, she is a fervent Methodist and disapproves of what she looks on as Popish ritual. So she sits on a chair at the entrance and will not enter the Chapel itself."

She looked at the Earl to see if he was listening to her.

"I slipped out by a side door and, as I will return by the same route, my maid will not be aware that I have visited you."

"I sincerely hope not!" the Earl exclaimed. "If this information was passed on to the Marquis, it would make things even worse than they are already."

Daphne wiped her tears from her eyes.

"Only *you* can save us both," she said. "I am sure that Arthur will be at home all the morning, but don't leave it too long or he may go to his Solicitors. Then he will refuse to see you and it will be too late."

The Earl felt as if he was dreaming and all of this could not in any way be true.

"And what about your stepdaughter?" he managed to ask. "Supposing she knows that I have been with you and tells her father that she has never even met me?"

"You can leave this to me," Daphne assured him. "All you have to do is to convince Arthur that you wish to marry his daughter."

As she spoke, Daphne glanced at the clock on the mantelpiece.

"I must go!" she exclaimed. "You had better let me out through the garden entrance into the Mews. It would be quicker than going out by the front door."

The Earl did not argue.

He merely opened the French window as Daphne pulled her veil back over her face.

Without speaking they walked quickly through the garden to where there was a door behind a clump of rhododendrons.

It could be opened without a key only from the inside.

The Earl opened it.

As he did so, Daphne looked up at him.

"I am so sorry, Norwin, that this has happened, but we have to save ourselves and this is the only way."

She did not wait for an answer, but turned from him and walked away.

The Earl could hear her footsteps as she ran down the cobbled surface of the Mews.

It was only a short distance to the Grosvenor Chapel and he thought that with any luck the Service would not be over before she arrived there.

As he shut the garden door and returned to his study, he wondered if he had imagined what he had just heard.

It could not be true! This could not really be happening to him!

But it had happened and he was committed because there was no other way out.

He had to ask the Marquis for his daughter's hand in marriage.

He did not even know what the girl looked like.

It was either that or what to him would be condemnation to an intolerable and unbearable existence.

Then, as he looked up at the sky, he said fervently as so many other men had before him,

'How in the Devil's name did I get myself into this horrendous mess?'

CHAPTER TWO

The Marchioness of Langbourne slipped into the Grosvenor Chapel and found that the Service was just finishing.

The congregation was moving towards the West door and she joined them and then saw her lady's maid waiting in the porch.

Without speaking she started walking as quickly as she could to Langbourne House in Park Street.

As she went in through the front door, the hands on the grandfather clock pointed to nine o'clock.

She had given orders before she went out that, since his Lordship was tired after his journey home from Paris, he was not to be called until nine o'clock with his breakfast.

She ran up the stairs and went to her stepdaughter's bedroom at the end of the corridor.

She entered the room without knocking and Sadira was standing at the window dressed in her riding habit.

She turned round as her stepmother entered and asked,

"Why was I told not to leave my room until you had spoken to me? I hear that Papa is back from France and I want to see him."

"Your father was very tired last night," the Marchioness replied, "and he has only just been called."

"Then can I go to him now?" Sadira asked her.

"Not until I have spoken to you," the Marchioness insisted.

She had closed the door behind her when she entered and now she walked across the room to stand in the window near to Sadira.

There was silence.

Then, as Sadira looked questioningly at her stepmother, the Marchioness began,

"Later this morning the Earl of Kensall will be calling on your father to ask if you and he can announce your engagement."

Sadira looked at her stepmother in sheer astonishment.

"What are you – saying?" she asked. "Whatever are you – talking about?"

"I am telling you," the Marchioness replied, "that you are to marry the Earl of Kensall."

Sadira drew in her breath.

"I will do nothing of the sort! I am not a fool, Stepmama! I know quite well that he has been seeing you almost every night that Papa has been away."

"You may know that," the Marchioness said coldly, "but you will not repeat it to your father.

You will tell him that you are delighted by the Earl's attentions and thrilled to be his wife."

"I think you must be crazy!" Sadira expostulated. "I have no wish to marry the Earl – in fact I would not marry him under any circumstances."

There was now a pause in the conversation and she was trying to speak without being offensively rude to her stepmother.

The Marchioness walked to an armchair and sat down wearily.

"Now, listen to me," she ordered. "Your father reviled me last night because of what his detective reported to him while he was away."

Sadira pressed her lips together as if she would say something and with an effort she remained silent.

"I told him," the Marchioness went on, "that he is entirely mistaken in what he assumed and that the Earl had come here to see *you*."

"That is a lie," Sadira contended. "And I don't believe for a moment that Papa could be so stupid as to believe it."

"I think I have convinced your father that he is mistaken and you therefore have to bail me out. When the Earl invites you to be his wife, you must accept with pleasure."

"Of course I will not!" Sadira fumed. "Do you really think, Stepmama, that I would be willing to marry a man who is infatuated with you?"

She paused for a minute to glare at the Marchioness.

"If you want to know the truth, I am greatly shocked at the way you have behaved in my father's absence."

"Whether you are shocked or not," the Marchioness retorted, "you will do as I say. Otherwise there will be an enormous scandal that will affect you as well as me and distress the whole family."

"If there is a scandal, it is all your doing," Sadira replied, "and I can only say that my mother would never have behaved in the way that you have."

The Marchioness leaned back in the chair.

"Are you saying," she said slowly, "that you will not support my explanation of what has happened and will refuse to marry the Earl of Kensall?"

"I will tell Papa the truth," Sadira persisted defiantly. "Whatever action he decides to take in this matter will be between you and him and so has nothing to do with me."

The Marchioness's eyes narrowed.

"Very well, if that is your attitude, then I shall make you suffer as I myself will suffer."

The way she spoke made Sadira look at her nervously.

"What are you – saying?" she asked.

"I remember you telling me when we were last in the country," the Marchioness said, "that you loved your horse, Swallow, and your dog, Bracken, more than anything else in the world."

"What have – they to do with it?" Sadira asked quickly.

"If you will not help me," the Marchioness replied, "I will have Swallow taken to a place where you cannot find him and he will be given nothing to eat and nothing to drink until he dies."

Sadira gave a cry of horror and her stepmother went on,

"I will take Bracken to the slums somewhere in the East End and give him to one of those hardened criminals who beat their dogs when they have had too much to drink."

"I – don't believe you!" Sadira cried. "Nobody could be so cruel or – so wicked as to treat – animals in such a way!"

"You can, of course, save them," the Marchioness declared coldly. "Otherwise I promise you I shall do what I say and they will suffer as I shall suffer if your father divorces me."

Sadira started.

"Papa intends to – divorce you?" she questioned.

"That is what he will do," the Marchioness replied, "unless you convince him that he is wrong in his assumptions and that you are delighted to make a brilliant social marriage to the Earl."

Her voice altered as she ranted at Sadira furiously,

"Don't be such a silly fool, girl! Every young woman in London has attempted to catch the Earl of Kensall. But he has remained a bachelor despite every effort that has been made to trap him into Matrimony."

"And now you think – you have succeeded," Sadira countered sarcastically.

"The Earl has accepted the situation and will call on your father some time this morning. If you are going riding, you will return in no more than an hour and, having changed, will be waiting for him."

Sadira turned towards the window as if she could not bear to look at her stepmother.

Then she said in a small voice that was very different from the way she had spoken before,

"Do I – have to do – this?"

"There is no alternative," the Marchioness said. "And make no mistake, if you are not convincing and your father does not believe you, then you will never see Swallow or Bracken again!"

She paused for breath before she went on,

"And don't think you will get away scot-free. If you ruin my life, I will ruin yours. There will be at least a little while before it becomes known what your father is doing."

She looked at Sadira to see if she was listening.

"In the meantime I shall make it my business to inform every hostess in London what you are really like."

"What – I am – really like?" Sadira exclaimed in surprise.

"I will tell them," the Marchioness continued, dropping her voice, "that your immoral behaviour has upset and distressed your father. That you have had clandestine affairs with the grooms who accompany you out riding and that I have had to dismiss two footmen because you made advances to them."

Sadira gave a cry of sheer horror while the Marchioness rattled on,

"You know as well as I do how such a story would circulate like a wild wind amongst the gossips of Mayfair."

She paused a moment and then went on harshly,

"You may deny it, you may try to live it down, but it will be repeated and repeated until, like your animals, you are in the grave!"

She almost spat the words at Sadira.

There was silence as Sadira looked out of the window with unseeing eyes.

The Marchioness rose to her feet.

"I am not making idle threats," she stressed. "My future life depends entirely on you, just as the lives of your horse and dog do."

There was no reply from Sadira.

Knowing that she had won the battle, the Marchioness flounced out of the room.

In her own bedroom she powdered her face until she looked very pale and then she deliberately drew a dark line under her eyes where none had been naturally.

She then changed from the dark gown that she had worn to go to the Church into one that was frilly and feminine.

It took her some time and, when she looked at the clock, she knew that the Marquis would now be dressing himself.

She went to his room and, after she had knocked on the door, it was opened by his valet.

The Marchioness passed by the man without speaking and he tactfully went into the corridor closing the door behind him.

Inside the room the Marchioness stood with her back to the door.

Her husband was dressed with the exception of his coat and he was brushing back the sides of his hair as he stood in front of the mirror.

It was going white and there was a bald patch on the back of his head.

He did not turn round and, when the Marchioness did not speak, he asked her in a hard voice,

"What do you want?"

"I – came," the Marchioness replied in a soft childlike voice, "to see if – you are still – angry with – m-me."

"What do you expect?" her husband replied.

"I-I have been – crying all night – because you did not – believe me."

"I am not a fool," the Marquis said, "and I have the evidence here to show me exactly how you behaved after I left to go to France."

"That is what – you said – last night," the Marchioness replied, "but I told you the truth – only you – refuse to believe me."

"As I said, I am not a fool," the Marquis answered.

The Marchioness came a little nearer to him.

"Please, Arthur, please – talk to Sadira and, of course, to the Earl of Kensall before you accuse me in this – way."

The Marquis put down his hairbrushes.

"Where is Sadira?" he asked. "Why has she not come to see me?"

"She wanted to, but was told that you were asleep and so went riding," the Marchioness said. "But she will be back in a short time and then you will know that I am telling – you the – truth."

She gave a little sob that was very effective.

"I love – you – I have always – loved you! How can you think I would look at any other man – except you?"

Her voice broke on the last words.

As if she could control her tears no longer, she turned and ran from the room.

She left the door open behind her so that the Marquis could hear her running down the corridor.

He sighed and picked up the detective's report. It was lying on the top of the chest of drawers. Putting it into his pocket, he walked slowly and heavily down the stairs to his study.

There was a large amount of paperwork waiting for him on his desk and, although he sat down in his comfortable writing chair, he did not touch any of it.

Instead he stared ahead with the eyes of a man who has received a body blow and finds it hard to bear the agony and humiliation of it.

*

The Earl of Kensall arrived at Langbourne House at exactly eleven o'clock.

It was just a short distance from his own house in Park Lane and, because it was a formal occasion, he travelled in one of his modern carriages.

He was dressed formally as well.

He told himself mockingly that he might be making a friendly call on the Marquis rather than going to his execution.

He could imagine nothing more appalling than being forced into Matrimony with a girl he had hardly seen or spoken to.

She would doubtless be fully aware that he was the lover of her stepmother.

If she was not aware of it, then she must be half-witted and indeed he suspected that most *debutantes* were.

He would therefore probably find her incredibly boring for the rest of his life.

As his horses swept him down the street, he tried to think of any possible way out of this appalling situation.

He carefully thought through all the possible solutions to his deadly dilemma and he could, however, find no sensible alternative to the Marchioness's devilish scheme.

Even to think of the horror of being subjected to protracted divorce proceedings made him shudder.

He could easily imagine how shocked all his relatives would be and his enemies would laugh heartily and claim that he had received his 'just deserts'.

Those who had always been jealous of him would be able to crow loudly in their pleasure at his predicament.

To live abroad would be, he recognised, a Hell on earth. How could he leave his estates, his racehorses, his hunters, his Clubs and all his friends?

He reached Langbourne House in plenty of time and looked at the pillared front door that he had entered surreptitiously so many times in the past few weeks.

As he did so, he knew that he hated Daphne Langbourne.

She herself had enticed him into the ignominious position that he now found himself in.

There was only one possible way that he could extricate himself and that was if he could lie convincingly enough to deceive the Marquis.

The shame and indignity of it all was almost too dreadful to comprehend.

He wanted to shout out to his footman, who had now jumped down to the pavement, that he had changed his mind and his carriage would drive on.

But then he would have no other recourse and the Marquis would surely go ahead with the divorce proceedings as he had threatened.

It might take many months and the gossips would talk of nothing else all over London, but the end was looming up at him inevitably.

And he would be exiled from everything that really mattered to him in his life.

His footman ran up the steps and rang the bell.

The door was then opened immediately, which told the Earl that he was most definitely expected.

Feeling that every step took him nearer to the guillotine, he descended from his carriage and walked into the hall.

"Good morning, my Lord," the butler greeted him respectfully.

With an effort the Earl forced himself to reply.

Without being asked whom he wished to see, which showed that Daphne had given her orders to the butler, he was led down the corridor to the study, which was a room that he knew well.

Daphne had always waited for him in the drawing room, which was a perfect frame for her beauty. Or else in her bedroom.

She had given him a key so that he could let himself into the house without, she believed, the servants being aware of it.

Now the Earl thought rather belatedly that it would have been wiser if she had let him in, perhaps through the garden gate at the back of the house.

The detective who had been watching him had obviously seen him enter and leave by the front door when everybody else in the house was supposedly asleep.

Now the butler opened the door of the study.

As he did so, the Earl thought that there was so much evidence against him that nothing he could say would make the Marquis believe anything but the truth.

As he entered, the Marquis rose from behind his desk.

At a quick glance the Earl thought that he was looking particularly aggressive.

He had also aged considerably since he had last seen him only a few weeks earlier and there were now deeply etched lines on his face that had not been there previously.

He could not help being aware that the older man was suffering considerably.

Only the Earl's strong self-control and the fact that he was virtually fighting for his life made him appear to be at ease as he faced the Marquis.

In what appeared to be a friendly and normal tone of voice he started the conversation that he had been dreading,

"Good morning, my Lord. It's good to see you back in London again and I feel sure that your mission to Paris has been as successful as the Prime Minister had hoped."

The Marquis moved from his desk to stand in front of the fireplace.

"I understand you wanted to see me, Kensall," he responded harshly.

"Yes, indeed," the Earl replied. "I have come to ask you for your permission to marry – Sadira."

There was a distinct pause before he enunciated the last word as for one rather terrifying moment the Earl in his anxiety had forgotten the girl's name!

The Marquis looked at him sharply.

"This surely is somewhat unexpected?"

"Not really. I fell in love with Sadira as soon as I saw her and we have been seeing each other every day while you have been awayin France."

He forced a somewhat crooked smile to his lips before he added,

"I think we will be very happy together, as we both have a passion for horses, which is a deep bond in common."

The Marquis then moved from where he had been standing in front of the fireplace and walked slowly across the room to the window.

With his back to the Earl he said as if he was carefully thinking out every word,

"Sadira is very young. It seems strange, in view of your reputation, that you should be interested in a girl who knows nothing of the Social world that you move around in."

"I can understand your point of view," the Earl said, "but surely you realise, my Lord, that what a man looks for in a wife is very different from what he finds enjoyable as a bachelor?"

There was a long silence and then the Marquis turned from the window.

"Is what you are saying to me the truth, Kensall?" he enquired. "Are you really in love with Sadira and will you make her the sort of husband that I would want for my daughter's future happiness?"

The Earl raised his eyebrows as if he was surprised by the Marquis's question.

"I cannot imagine, my Lord, why you should suspect that I am telling you anything but the truth," he answered, "or why you should question my desire to make your daughter my wife."

He thought as he spoke that he was being rather subtle in taking the initiative.

It was better than maintaining a somewhat defensive role as he sensed that the Marquis was fighting a strong desire to accuse him outright of having seduced his wife.

He was therefore determined that, if it was at all possible, such words would not be spoken as it would open up a chasm that Daphne and he would fall straight into.

"What I am asking," he resumed briskly, "is that you will allow us to announce our engagement and plan our Wedding for later in the year."

He paused for a moment to clear his throat and then continued,

"I realise that Sadira is very young and I would not want to deprive her of attending the many balls that are taking place during the Season."

He gave a short laugh and added,

"She is entitled to them, although I must say they bore me. But we want to be together and, of course, it is easy while we are both in London."

Again there was a long uncomfortable silence that made the Earl feel apprehensive and uneasy.

With an obvious effort the Marquis now said slowly,

"I will talk to Sadira and, if her wishes prove to be the same as yours, then, of course, I must agree."

"Thank you, my Lord! Thank you very much indeed!" the Earl said with an air of affected gaiety.

He had been afraid ever since he had entered the room that the Marquis would express in no uncertain terms what was uppermost in his mind.

"Now that you have given me your permission," the Earl tried to smile, "perhaps I could see Sadira and tell her the good news?"

The Marquis then walked across to his desk and, picking up a small gold bell, rang it vigorously.

The door was opened at once and, as the butler appeared, he ordered,

"Send Lady Sadira to me."

"Very good, my Lord."

The two men were alone again and the Earl said conversationally,

"I hope to have a winner tomorrow at Kempton Park. Will you be attending the Meeting, my Lord?"

"I don't know," the Marquis replied in a tired voice. "I had not expected to be in London for another week."

The Earl realised that this was dangerous ground as he might now be told the reason why the Marquis had hurried home at such speed.

"Well, if you do go," he said swiftly, "I suggest you put a small amount on Triumph, which I am running in the second race and there is a good chance that I shall be successful in the fourth race with a horse called Lightning."

The Marquis did not reply and the Earl went on speaking rapidly,

"This will be the first time he has been tried out in a big race. I have great faith in him and I would value your opinion after you have seen him run."

The Marquis had by now moved back to his desk and he was looking down at something that lay in front of him on his blotter.

The Earl suspected that it was the detective's report covering Daphne's movements while he had been away. And it was this that had brought him hurrying home from France to face his wife.

The Marquis did not pick up the paper, he merely stared morosely at it.

As he did so, the door opened and Sadira came into the room.

As he looked at her, the Earl was astonished.

He had, in fact, no set idea of what she might look like.

He had suspected that, if she took after her father, she would be tall, heavily-built and perhaps passably good-looking but not at all outstanding.

Instead, he saw a slim sylph-like figure.

As he glanced at her face, he knew that she was completely different in every way from any woman he had seen or met before.

There was no doubt that she was beautiful and yet there was nothing conventional about her looks.

Her hair was fair, but of a colour that resembled the rays of the sun when it first rose over the horizon in the morning.

Her skin had the translucence of a pearl and her eyes were blue, but not the conventional blue of an English beauty. They were the blue of the Madonna's robe and as brilliant as the Mediterranean Sea. And so especially large that they seemed in fact to dominate her small pointed face.

There was a sensitivity about her that surprised the Earl.

And he realised that it was something that he had never seen before.

As their eyes met, he was aware at once, without her having to say so, that she both hated and despised him.

Sadira looked away from him towards her father.

And then she ran to the desk and put her arms round the Marquis's neck.

"You are back home. Papa!" she exclaimed. "I have missed you so much. Did you enjoy yourself in Paris?"

The words seemed to come quite spontaneously to her lips.

The Earl, however, was immediately aware that she was acting her part as well as he had acted his.

"I came back," the Marquis replied to her slowly, "for reasons that we need not discuss. I understand from the Earl of Kensall that he wishes to make you his wife. Do you want to marry him?"

Sadira forced a smile to her lips.

"Has he told you the news, Papa? I do hope you are pleased."

Listening to her the Earl thought that she had avoided her father's question rather cleverly.

"I suppose," the Marquis said, "if that is what you want, I must give you my blessing and hope that you will both be very happy together."

There was an unmistakable note of doubt in the last words, but Sadira ignored it.

She merely kissed her father again and then said,

"Dearest Papa, there is a great deal to plan and to talk about, but, if you will allow us to become engaged, there is no need to worry about the Wedding yet."

The Marquis rose from his chair.

"I assume," he said, "that you wish to celebrate the decision you have made, so I will go and select something that is appropriate to drink your health with."

He did not sound at all elated about it and then he went from the room, closing the door somewhat sharply behind him.

Sadira stood very still, as if she was turned to stone and then she looked at the Earl.

"I must commend you," he said, "on playing your part very skilfully."

"As I imagine you played yours," she retorted.

"There was nothing else we could do," the Earl said grimly.

"Nothing," Sadira agreed.

She was thinking as she spoke of how her stepmother had diabolically threatened to destroy her beloved horse and her dog.

She wondered if she had thought up anything so effective but cruel herself or whether the idea had come from the Earl.

She was not yet a part of the Social world, but she was well aware that for someone in her stepmother's elevated position to be forced to go through the Divorce Courts was to sink into the gutter.

Sadira had been very young at the time, but she could remember the endless gossip there had been when the Prince of Wales had been cited as a co-respondent in the scandalous Mordaunt divorce case back in 1870.

For weeks nobody had talked about anything else and their voices had seemed to grow louder and louder as every titbit of information was relayed and then repeated a thousand times until the newspapers could find something even more sensational for the public to devour.

The Prince of Wales had defended himself and he had come out of the case officially without a stain on his character.

But nobody at the time wanted to believe that it was the truth.

Sadira could well remember her Governess saying to the housekeeper,

"He's got away with it, the lucky Prince, but who is going to believe it?"

She knew that her father must not be involved in a divorce case that would be equally notorious and damaging for all involved especially him.

It would strike horribly at his pride and the dignity that she had always admired him for.

She supposed that the same could be said of the Earl and she was well aware that he was spoken of as the most handsome and attractive bachelor in all of Society as well as being the wealthiest.

Because she was so interested in horses, she had followed his career on the Racecourse with great interest and she knew exactly how many winners he had in his stables.

She was also sure that her stepmother was wildly and passionately in love with him.

The Marchioness could not contain her excitement when she was able to see him without her husband being aware of it.

Sadira was too astute not to realise that there had been other men in her stepmother's life, but she had never attached much importance to them and they had never lasted very long anyway.

In fact she was prepared to ignore them as long as they did not interfere with her father's happiness.

He did not see the irrepressible radiance in his wife's face when she knew that he was going away for a few days. He might miss it because he was getting old, but Sadira noticed it at once.

She hated her stepmother and despised her for her infidelity and, when she thought of how she had taken her mother's place, she wanted to cry.

Yet, because she was intelligent, she understood that her father needed a woman at his side.

She had to admit too that her stepmother had made her father happy and, because she was so beautiful, he was proud of her.

Now Sadira thought of the scenario of herself being married to a man who loved another woman and that woman was none other than her own stepmother.

It was an utter humiliation that made her feel as if she would never be able to hold up her head again.

She then walked from behind the desk to stand a little nearer to the Earl.

She was afraid that anyone outside in the corridor might hear what they were saying. It was certainly not because she wanted to be close to him.

"I suppose," she suggested in a low voice, "it is possible for us to remain engaged for some months – and then I could refuse to marry you at the last moment?"

The Earl did not answer her at first.

And then at last he said,

"We could, of course, try it, but I rather fancy that your father, having accepted me as his son-in-law, will insist on our marriage if only to convince himself that the unpleasant report he had commissioned does not tell the true story."

Sadira knew exactly what he was saying and she thought in a way that he was more astute than she had expected.

She knew that her father would find it difficult if not impossible to forget altogether what had made him return to England so precipitately.

He would therefore be carefully watching them and so any attempt to terminate their engagement would undoubtedly arouse his suspicions.

He might even then seek to divorce his wife and cite the Earl as the co-respondent.

It all passed rapidly through her mind.

As it did so, she realised that the Earl was thinking the same as her.

"Then what can we – do?" she asked anxiously.

"Nothing," the Earl answered.

"But – there must be – some way out?"

He shook his head.

"I doubt it. The detective's evidence would be very convincing and even now I am quite certain that your father is suspicious that we are not as interested in each other as we are pretending to be."

Sadira put her hands up to her face.

The words that came to her lips were, she knew, so offensive that she dared not say them.

Instead she sat down at her father's desk and, without consciously doing so, she unfolded the piece of paper that lay on top of the blotter.

Only as she looked at it did she realise what it was.

It was in the form of a diary and there were notes against each day as to what time the Earl had entered the house after dark and what time he had left.

She looked at it with an expression of disgust on her face and he then realised what she was reading.

He walked quickly to the desk and picked up the piece of paper and one glance at it told him that his suspicions were correct.

"There is no reason for you to read this," he said angrily, "and the sooner it is forgotten the better."

"*You* may be able to forget it," Sadira answered coldly, "but I assure you it is something I shall never forget – nor will I ever forgive you."

"It would be better to try," the Earl suggested. "Otherwise we have no chance of even attempting to make the best of a bad job."

"You can try, my Lord, but I hate and despise you for hurting my father and, of course, for spoiling any chance I may have of happiness in my own life in the future."

It did flash through the Earl's mind that most young women would be perfectly content to marry him whatever his reputation.

He found it hard to believe that this beautiful girl should be so antagonistic.

She looked like a piece of Dresden china or as if she had stepped down out of a picture by Botticelli.

Men of his age were expected to have indulged in numerous love affairs before they led their bride down the aisle and, if she had any inkling of what her bridegroom had done in the past, she would choose to forget it.

It would be easy to do so in the light of having an unassailable position in Society and in the case of someone like himself of having a great deal of money to spend and magnificent houses to live in.

But Sadira was looking at him intently with her unusual blue eyes.

He had the uncomfortable feeling that she was telling the truth and she would neither forget nor forgive.

"Now, listen to me," he urged. "We are both aware that this is a very unfortunate situation to find ourselves in – "

He stopped a moment before continuing,

"But if we are sensible, we can start by being friends. I am sure we will find that we have a great number of interests in common, horses for one."

Sadira did not answer or move and he went on,

"You are very young and therefore, like most young women, you see everything in black or white. What we all have to do in life is to accept that there is good and bad in everyone and it is always very much more comfortable to ignore the bad."

"You are very plausible, my Lord," Sadira answered, "and I will certainly consider what you have said. At the same time I find it difficult to make – excuses for the Devil."

She spoke softly but clearly and the Earl could not think of an immediate answer.

Then, before he could do say anything at all, the door opened.

The Marquis returned, followed by his butler carrying a silver tray with a bottle of champagne on it.

CHAPTER THREE

The Earl put down his empty glass.

"I have an appointment shortly," he said, "so I must leave you now. But I will return this afternoon with an engagement ring, which I am certain that Sadira will cherish as my mother cherished hers when she received it from my father."

He was hoping as he spoke that he sounded like a man in love.

Now for the first time there was a faint smile on the Marquis's lips as he said,

"If you are coming back here, Kensall, then I suggest you stay for dinner."

What that meant flashed through the Earl's and Sadira's mind at the same moment. That nothing could be more uncomfortable than to have to dine with the Marchioness.

Only very quick thinking enabled the Earl to reply,

'It is most kind of you, my Lord, but I am sure you will understand that it is very important that my grandmother should meet Sadira and hear the good news before any other members of my family. And I would like to take Sadira to dine with her this evening."

'In that case," the Marquis nodded, "I must withdraw my invitation."

He was beginning to look more cheerful and the Earl thought that he was at least three-quarters of the way to being convinced that what they had told him was the truth.

"I will come to see you tomorrow," he went on, "but, if you have time this afternoon, please put the announcement of our engagement in *The London Gazette* and *The Times*."

He stopped speaking to look at the Marquis.

"I will then notify all the most significant members of the Kensall family during the afternoon," he concluded.

"I will do as you suggest," the Marquis replied, "and, of course, my daughter can help me."

The Earl turned to Sadira.

"Goodbye until this evening and I will call for you at about seven o'clock."

"That will be lovely," Sadira managed to reply with what sounded rather like genuine enthusiasm in her voice.

The Marquis was watching them and, as the Earl moved towards the door, he said to his daughter,

"You had better see your young man out, as I suspect that he will want to have a last word alone with you."

"Of course, Papa."

Sadira then went out of the study with the Earl, closing the door behind them.

"That was clever of you," she said in a low voice.

"I really do want you to meet my grandmother," he replied, "and I will send a note to her immediately, telling her that we will be with her at seven-thirty. You will understand that she dines early."

"Of course," Sadira answered.

They had reached the hall by now where the butler was waiting for them.

"I will have to hurry," the Earl said. "It is always a mistake to keep the Prime Minister waiting."

"Yes, but tell your coachman to drive carefully," Sadira cautioned.

"I will," the Earl replied.

He then hurried out through the front door held open by a footman who bowed reverently to him.

As Sadira walked slowly up the stairs, she felt that they had now convinced everyone, including the servants, of their relationship.

Then, as she went to her own room, she wondered to herself desperately how she could do this.

How was it possible for her to marry a man she hated and despised, a man who she knew had no wish to marry her?

'What – can I – do? *What can – I do?*' she murmured under her breath.

Because she did not want under any circumstances to encounter her stepmother, she stayed in her bedroom until luncheontime.

Then, as she heard the gong being sounded by the butler, she reluctantly went down the stairs.

Her father and stepmother were just coming from the study.

"Oh, there, you are, Sadira," the Marquis said. "I was just relating the good news to your stepmother and, of course, she is delighted."

Sadira thought that there was a slight touch of sarcasm in his voice.

Before she could respond to her father, the Marchioness exclaimed gushingly,

"Oh, dearest Sadira! What wonderful news! I am so happy for you and I cannot think of anyone who would grace the position of the Countess of Kensall better than yourself."

"Thank you," Sadira replied. "I thought you would be pleased and I know that I am very very lucky."

She tried to speak convincingly as if she was a young girl swept off her feet by the first love in her life.

They went into luncheon after the butler had announced it and the Marchioness talked endlessly of the large trousseau that Sadira would need and the sooner they started shopping for it the better.

Sadira could see across the table that her father was listening to the Marchioness and all her suggestions.

At the very same time her instinct told her that he still half-suspected that he was being deceived.

She therefore put out her hand to touch his.

"Stepmama is going too fast," she said. "While I am thrilled and delighted to be engaged to Norwin, I do *not* wish to have to leave home too soon. You know, Papa, I am always happy when I am with you."

The Marquis's eyes softened.

"And I love having you with me, my dearest, but I must accept that it will be impossible now that you will be preoccupied most of the time, as you surely will be, with your fiancé."

"I still want to be with you every moment of the day that you can spare for me," Sadira insisted.

Somehow they managed to get through the meal and Sadira felt as if she was walking a tightrope and at any moment she might slip and fall into a chasm below.

She had no idea what she ate and she noticed that, when her stepmother was not being over-gushing, she was looking at her with a hard look in her eyes.

'She hates me as much as I hate her,' Sadira thought. 'How could Papa have married such a ghastly woman in the first place?'

She thought that the only consolation in having to marry the Earl would be to get away from the Marchioness's evil presence and she felt as though the whole house was poisoned by it.

After luncheon the Marchioness suggested that she might like to go shopping.

Sadira replied, however, that she had a good number of letters to write.

"I suppose you want to tell your friends that you have beaten them to the matrimonial post?" her father commented in a strained effort at being humorous.

"You are quite right, Papa," Sadira replied, "and I just know that they will all want to be bridesmaids."

"I am sure they will," he agreed, "and they will be grinding their teeth all the way up the aisle!"

Sadira managed a rather stifled laugh as she could not help thinking that it was what she herself would be doing even louder than anyone else.

Her father had, however, put a good idea into her head.

So she decided that she would go to see her closest and dearest friend, Anne Beecham.

They had known each other since childhood and they had shared a Governess for several years and had then gone to the same Finishing School.

Anne was a great deal more intelligent than most of their contemporaries and she had therefore at school shared with Sadira the extra Tutors whom the Marquis had ordered for her.

Feeling that she must talk to someone, Sadira reckoned that the only person she could trust would be Anne.

They were very close to each other and often remarked that they were just like sisters.

She knew that nothing she told Anne would be passed on to anybody else.

Equally she was nervous about hearing Anne's reactions to anything as unpleasant and sordid as the position she found herself in at the moment.

Although she had known of her stepmother's infidelity, she had never told Anne about it and she had tried to pretend even to herself that it was not happening in her supposedly happy home.

Because she loved her father, she had prayed that he would never know as he would be intolerably humiliated by all the intrigue and deception.

Now she had been forced to save the Earl and her father from being involved in a divorce case.

She wondered if it was really to her father's advantage to have to live for the rest of his life with a woman who was nothing more than what people in Society would call, 'a common whore'.

'I just cannot think clearly while I am in the same house with her,' Sadira told herself morbidly.

She rang the bell for her maid.

When she came, Sadira told her to order a carriage and that she was to accompany her.

"I am visiting a friend," she told her.

Unlike the Marquis Anne's parents, Lord and Lady Beecham, spent most of their time in London.

They went to the country only when they stayed with friends and, because Anne, like Sadira, loved riding, she had greatly enjoyed staying at Langbourne Hall.

She rode the Marquis's horses and did everything else that Sadira enjoyed to the full.

They had even planned how often they could be together during the Season when they were both to be *debutantes*.

Lord Beecham was giving a ball for Anne and the Marquis was giving one for Sadira.

They were both to be presented at their first 'Drawing Room' to Queen Victoria at Buckingham Palace.

And, as they would be invited to the same balls, their parents could take it in turns to give dinner parties for them.

'I must see Anne,' Sadira determined, 'only she will understand and help me through my darkest hour.'

*

A short while later Sadira was driving towards Anne's house.

She was turning over in her mind exactly what she should say.

'I will tell her the truth,' she decided, 'and Anne I am certain will surely understand.'

At the same time she shuddered from actually putting into words the horror that she felt at her stepmother's behaviour.

She also shrank from explaining to her the degrading position that she had been forced to accept in order to deceive her father.

She knew that Anne would be as shocked at the whole situation as she was herself.

The carriage drew up outside Lady Beecham's delighful house in Belgrave Square.

Only then did Sadira think that perhaps it would be a mistake to tell Anne the whole sordid truth.

It would be better on the whole just to say that her father and stepmother had arranged her marriage without consulting her.

But, of course, she was pleased at having such a splendid and influential bridegroom!

When the front door opened, she realised that she was not the first visitor.

In the hall were men's top hats and a number of elegant sunshades, which told her that Lady Beecham was entertaining.

"Good afternoon, my Lady," the butler, who naturally knew her well, greeted her.

"Good afternoon, Watkins," Sadira replied. "What is happening today?"

"Her Ladyship is holding a meeting here, my Lady, of one of her Charities to help the heathens."

Sadira's spirits sank.

She knew only too well that Anne's mother was a very religious woman and she spent a great deal of her time and money in helping charitable causes.

On one occasion Sadira had been dragged in to help make what were known as 'mother Hubbards.

These were, she remembered, very ugly dresses from one of the African countries, where the children were naked and their mothers were in very much the same condition most of the time.

When Sadira stayed with Anne, she had to be down early for breakfast because Family Prayers always took place in the dining room every day before breakfast was brought in.

All the staff were expected to attend and either Lord or Lady Beecham presided.

They read the Collect of the day followed by a number of prayers that the congregation were expected to reply to with fervent Amens.

Now, as Sadira seemed indecisive, the butler suggested,

"If I were you, my Lady, I'd slip into the back of the room and, when Miss Anne sees you, she'll come away as quick as possible."

"That is a good idea," Sadira smiled at him.

The butler led the way to the dining room and Sadira knew that by now it would be filled with chairs all neatly arranged in rows.

They would face towards a table at the end of the room where Lady Beecham and the organisers of the Charity would be seated. There would not be a large audience, if it was anything like the meetings that she had attended before.

Those who were there would all be middle-aged or elderly friends who came because Lady Beecham asked them to. Another reason was that they knew that after the meeting was over there would be an excellent tea. And this would take place in the drawing room.

Sadira thought that, when the audience started to move away from the breakfast room, she and Anne could escape upstairs.

They could talk in what had once been the schoolroom but was now her friends' sitting room.

Watkins opened the door quietly and Sadira walked past him into a vacant chair that was right at the back.

As she did so, she was aware that a soberly dressed man was giving a lecture and she was not surprised to find that it was about North Africa.

It was a part of the world that Lady Beecham was particularly interested in.

Sadira had learned a considerable amount in the past about Africa from various Charities that Lady Beecham generously supported.

Now she noticed that the man speaking had white hair and a kind face and he spoke in a deep positive voice.

He was describing a camel market in Marocco and making it easy for the audience to imagine the men with their array of great beasts.

He told them in detail of the women sitting on the sand and selling homemade goods or twirling wool into yarn on hand spinners.

"They use," he said, "big skeins of coarse stuff, while the baby camels nuzzle against their mothers."

He then went on to describe how hard the women were forced to work and how difficult it was for most of them to feed their children and even keep alive.

To her surprise Sadira then found herself deeply interested in what he was saying.

This speaker most certainly knew his subject well and he spoke with an unmistakable air of sincerity.

Having heard so many of them, Sadira had learnt to tell which speakers were genuinely concerned with the Charity that they were raising funds for, while others merely repeated what they had read in pamphlets or had been told to say.

The man with white hair went on to speak about the lack of available medical help. It led, he said, to a great deal of unnecessary suffering especially amongst the women.

"It's not only a question of medical supplies," he went on, "but the knowledge of those who administer them is very limited and many children die because there is no one who can tell their mothers how to treat even the commonest illnesses."

He paused to look round his audience before he continued,

"The women themselves as well frequently have an agonising time in childbirth."

He told his listeners how the countries of North Africa were still entirely a man's world and the women had to keep their faces covered and waited on their husbands at meals. They were then allowed to eat what was left after their husbands had finished.

Another urgent need, he declared, was any sort of schools for the children.

Trained technicians were desperately lacking as well in everything that concerned the economic development of the region.

"I am," he proclaimed with a faint smile, "just a voice crying in the wilderness. To send out Medical Missionaries like myself costs money and that is not available unless people like your good selves are warm-hearted enough to help us, not only with your prayers but also from your purses."

He then sat down and there was rather more applause than would be usual on such an occasion.

Lady Beecham, who had been listening intently to him, then rose to her feet.

"I know you will want me to thank Father Christopher," she began, "for his excellent address and for all we have learned about the poor women of North Africa. I need not ask you to give generously to his cause because I know you will do so."

She paused to look at the audience and then continued,

"Father Christopher will be leaving England in two days' time and I feel certain that we would want to send him back with enough money to help at least some of the wretched women and children who are suffering so badly in North Africa."

She was about to say something more, when Father Christopher, who had just sat down, rose to his feet again.

"I think we should make it clear, my Lady, so that there is no mistake," he said, "that while I spoke of North Africa in general this afternoon, I am in fact, when I leave England, going first to Morocco."

He paused and then added,

"I am told that I am urgently needed in what to the Muslims is the Sacred City of Fez and I know that all I have said this afternoon applies specially to that beautiful country."

He sat down to more applause and Lady Beecham rose again to say,

"You know, Father, that we wish to help you wherever you go. Your wonderful work has already been commented on by Her Majesty the Queen and we know that any money we give you will be spent in the best and most effective way."

Father Christopher nodded as if in agreement and Lady Beecham then added,

"I hope now that you will all come to the drawing room for tea and, of course, to talk to Father Christopher personally. Any donations you feel able to give us will be collected at the door."

Those who were seated at the table rose to be followed by those in the audience.

As they did so, they all started talking at once so that the room seemed to vibrate to the sound of it.

Anne, who had seen Sadira come into the room, joined her.

"Let's disappear while we can," she whispered.

They slipped out through the door before anybody else had reached it and then, running through the hall, they hurried up the stairs to Anne's sitting room.

As they reached it, Anne exclaimed,

"I am so glad to see you, Sadira. What has been happening? Have you been asked to any parties yet? Believe it or not I have had three invitations already."

Sadira drew in her breath before she said,

"I have something to tell you, Anne, dearest."

"What is it?" her friend asked.

"Papa has arranged that I am to – marry – the Earl of – Kensall."

Anne stared at her in astonishment.

"Marry – the Earl of Kensall?" she repeated after a moment. "But I had no idea that you even knew him."

"I know him now," Sadira answered, "and my engagement to him is being announced tomorrow."

"I don't believe it!" Anne exclaimed. "How can it all have happened so quickly? You never said a word to me about it when we met the day before yesterday."

"I did not – know it – myself then," Sadira replied.

"And he has asked you to marry him?" Anne asked as if she was trying to work it out for herself. "But, surely, this has all happened too quickly? How can you know if you really are in love with him?"

They had often insisted to each other that they would never marry until they were really in love and Sadira knew that this was what Anne was referring to.

Before Sadira could think of a reply, Anne added,

"I suppose, because your father is so grand, that you are being treated like Royalty and are having an arranged marriage! Oh, Sadira, we always promised each other that we would never agree to a marriage like that!"

"I – know," Sadira answered. "But Papa thinks that the Earl of Kensall – is different from other men."

"Which, of course, he is," Anne remarked. "I have heard about him because everybody says how handsome he is. Once Papa made some remark about his love affairs, but Mama said 'hush' and put her fingers up to her lips because I was present."

She had said all this before she put her hand up to her mouth as if to stop herself.

"Oh, dearest," she cried, "I am sorry. I should not have said that to you. But it is such a surprise! I thought we were going to spend at least half the Season together before either of us even thought about becoming engaged."

"I – know," Sadira answered, "but it is something I – cannot do – anything about. I just wanted you to – know about it before the announcement – appears in *The Gazette*."

Anne rose and kissed her friend.

"I love you, Sadira," she said, "and you know that the one thing I want is for you to be happy. If you are, it is all that matters."

Sadira wanted to say that she was miserably unhappy and that was why she had called to see her.

But she knew that it would be a mistake to say any such thing and there was nothing that Anne could do anyway except to commiserate with her.

She suddenly decided that she did not want to talk about it any further. The whole idea of it was too appalling to discuss.

If they talked and talked, as most women did, it could only make everything worse and it was bad enough as it was.

Impulsively she asked,

"I will tell you what I would like, Anne. I would like to meet Father Christopher. I was very interested in what he was saying. Perhaps after that we could come up here again and I can tell you more about my engagement."

"Of course, if that is what you would wish, dearest," Anne agreed, "and naturally I want to hear everything – about your – future."

She hesitated over the last words of her sentence.

Sadira was aware, because they knew each other so well, that Anne suspected that there was something wrong.

She was, however, too tactful to say so. She only took Sadira by the hand and they went slowly down the stairs that they had just run up so quickly.

Lady Beecham's large and attractive drawing room was full of the people who had attended the meeting.

There was a delicious tea laid out at one end of the room and a number of maids and footmen to serve it and they carried round every sort of sandwich, scone, biscuit and cake.

The Beechams were well known for their outstanding hospitality.

But Sadira knew that most of those present at Lady Beecham's invitation to support good works came because of the food rather than the cause.

Lady Beecham was a rather stout woman who had once been extremely pretty like her daughter.

She greeted Sadira with affection,

"How sweet of you, dear child, to come and help me," she gushed. "We have had one of the best meetings I can remember."

"I would like to meet Father Christopher," Sadira then asked her.

"Of course," Lady Beecham replied.

She took Sadira by the hand and drew her towards Father Christopher. He was talking to several ladies who appeared to be paying him fulsome compliments.

Lady Beecham swept them to one side.

"I want you to meet, Father," she said, "my daughter's great friend, Lady Sadira Bourne, whose father is the Marquis of Langbourne. She was just telling me how interested she was in your splendid talk on the many problems of North Africa."

The Father held out his hand.

"I rather like to think," he replied, "that I am not too prosy for the young these days."

Sadira laughed.

"Of course not! I thought that you painted in words a very eloquent picture of what is happening in a country that I have longed to visit."

The Missionary smiled at her.

"Then it is something you must certainly do when you have the opportunity."

"I have always wanted to go to Morocco," Sadira went on. "Have you been there many times before?"

"Several years ago," he replied, "and they have asked me particularly to visit them again. There are, I am led to believe, a number of Christians in the Old City of Fez, who are feeling neglected."

"Then I am sure that they will be delighted to see you, Father, especially as you are a Medical Missionary."

She remembered hearing that Medical Missionaries were far more respected than those who simply tried to wean the natives from one religion to theirs.

The difficulty was to find enough men prepared to spend four years on medical training when they thought it unnecessary as all they wanted to do was to preach the Gospel with great fervour.

"Are you going to Marocco alone or are other Missionaries going with you?" Sadira then asked him.

"On this occasion I am going alone," Father Christopher replied, "but I always hope that I shall acquire a disciple who will allow me to teach him in practice rather than learning it in a classroom."

Sadira smiled.

"I can understand and I should have thought that there were hundreds of students who would prefer to be 'in the fray' so to speak, rather than just swotting it up in books."

Father Christopher laughed heartily.

"You describe it very eloquently. But you would be surprised how difficult it is to get young men to accept training during what they think of as 'the best years of their lives' rather than riding into battle to fight negligence and neglect."

Anne, who was standing beside Sadira, chuckled at this remark.

"I rather sympathise with them," she said. "But if I was a man, I would come with you, Father Christopher."

"And I am sure that you would be a very great help. But I know that you would find the ship that I am travelling in to Tangier very uncomfortable."

Father Christopher paused and, with his eyes twinkling, added,

"Instead you must help me by getting your friends, like Lady Sadira, to remember that, while they curtsey to Her Majesty the Queen in Buckingham Palace, there are those in the world outside who are often very hungry and distressed."

"I will," Anne said simply, "and I know that Sadira will help me."

"You have an Arab name, Lady Sadira," Father Christopher now told her. "It means 'from the water'."

"I did not know its meaning, but my father chose it because he loves to travel and he much enjoyed Africa when he visited it."

"Then I feel that I am justified in asking you to remember that land," Father Christopher said, "and especially the people I shall be tending in Morocco."

"I will do," Sadira promised. "Anne and I will force our friends to be generous even when they don't want to be!"

Father Christopher shook his head.

"What is given willingly is more acceptable to God."

Some other people came up to speak to him and Anne turned to Sadira,

"I am sure that we can collect some of the money he requires."

"I will ask Papa for a donation tonight," Sadira replied. "As you know, he is always very generous."

"So is my father, if I can get him in the right mood," Anne said. "Do you want to talk to anybody else?"

"No, not really," Sadira answered, "and I think, after all, I should now go home. Papa arrived back from Paris only yesterday and I have hardly seen him."

She knew that this was an excuse that Anne would understand as she was well aware of how Sadira loved being with her father.

"Come and see me tomorrow," Anne proposed. "I want to show you my new gown that I am to be presented in. It's absolutely beautiful and Mama spent a fortune on it!"

"I have not yet had a chance to go shopping," Sadira admitted.

"Whatever you wear, you will look simply marvellous," Anne declared enthusiastically.

"I might say the same to you," Sadira countered.

Anne was very pretty, but her looks did not compare in any way with the unusual beauty of her friend.

Aloud she said,

"If I am told that anyone at Buckingham Palace looks lovelier than you, Sadira, I shall not believe it!"

"You may be quite certain that we will not eclipse any of the sophisticated beauties," Sadira replied. "They will make us appear very small fry."

She found herself thinking that the one person who would really try very hard to outshine her would be her stepmother.

*

Driving back in the carriage after leaving Anne, Sadira suddenly felt depressed.

She knew that the Marchioness would try to eclipse her not only at Buckingham Palace. She would do so every day in every way when they were at home.

Sadira was not so foolish as not to know that, while it was for her stepmother's benefit that she was saving the Earl from the Divorce Courts, the Marchioness was fiercely resenting her.

This was because, to do so, Sadira was marrying the man whom she herself loved.

'She hates me,' Sadira reasoned to herself, 'as she always has. And now, as I am taking her place in becoming the Earl's wife, she will want to kill me as well.'

She could understand in a way the agony that the Marchioness would suffer when she bore the Earl's name.

She would be consumed with jealousy when they went away on their honeymoon and when she sat at the opposite end of his table.

What was more, it was a hatred, Sadira ruminated, that would be echoed by the Earl himself.

If he loved her stepmother as he obviously did, he too would suffer, especially when he was forced to introduce her to Society as his wife.

And when he had to behave politely towards her in the presence of other people, when he saw her wearing the Kensall diamonds as his mother had and when she received his guests in his different houses.

Hatred, hatred, *hatred*!

In a mysterious way she could feel it vibrating all around her and she thought that it would be impossible to live in a world where there was no love and no friendship.

'I cannot bear it – I cannot live – like that,' Sadira told herself.

The carriage had by now reached the house in Park Street.

As she walked in through the front door, her stepmother came out from her father's study.

She looked at Sadira with suspicion in her eyes before she demanded,

"Where have you been? You did not tell me you were going out!"

Sadira did not answer.

The Marchioness then reached out and, grabbing her by the arm, dragged her into the nearest room.

She slammed the door shut and then stormed,

"How dare you leave this house without telling me where you were going! If you have been to visit Norwin, I can tell you here and now that he has no wish to have you running after him. The best thing you can do is to keep out of his way."

Sadira stared at the Marchioness in astonishment.

It had never entered her mind that her stepmother would think that she was running after the Earl.

Now she could see the fury in her eyes and the bitter contortion of her lips!

As she spoke so scathingly and offensively, Sadira realised that she was consumed with jealousy.

In a cold voice she replied,

"I have not been to see – the Earl of Kensall. And if I had, I hardly think you are the right person to reproach me for doing – your dirty work for you!"

With a cry of fury her stepmother reached out and slapped Sadira viciously across the face.

"How dare you speak to me like that!" she raged. "You are lucky, very lucky to be able to marry such a man. At the same time don't forget that it is me he loves – *me* – not *you*!"

As if her fury made it impossible for her to say anything more, the Marchioness turned and stalked out of the room.

She slammed the door behind her so violently that the china ornaments rattled around the room..

Sadira stood very still.

She could feel the sting of her stepmother's hand on her cheek, but she did not touch it.

She only told herself that this was a dreadful situation that she could not and would not endure.

CHAPTER FOUR

The Earl called at her house to take Sadira out to dinner and rather surprisingly he was late.

When he finally arrived, he did not climb out of his carriage.

He told the footman to inform her Ladyship that he was sorry he had been delayed and asked that she come and join him as quickly as she could.

Sadira was already waiting and she hurried into the hall and the butler put her velvet wrap over her shoulders.

Only as she pulled herself into the carriage beside the Earl did she realise that he was being very clever.

He obviously had no wish to see her stepmother and, by coming for her ten minutes late, he had the perfect excuse to say that they must hurry away immediately.

He put out his hand to take hers as she sat down beside him.

"I apologise," he said, "and I know you will understand that my grandmother is a very punctual person."

"Just like my mother," Sadira answered.

They drove off and the Earl was silent until they had nearly reached his grandmother's house, which was in Wilton Crescent.

Then he said,

"My grandmother was very kind to me when I was a boy and I know that you will convince her that we are going to be very happy. It would make her miserable if she thought that I was not."

"I understand," Sadira answered coldly.

She thought as she spoke how infuriating it was to have to act this part with everyone she met.

Then, as the candlelight in the carriage illuminated her hair and her face, the Earl asked her unexpectedly,

"What have you done to your cheek?"

For a moment she did not know what he meant.

Then, when she saw him looking at where the Marchioness had struck her, she felt her anger rise at the memory of the assault.

For a moment she was tempted to retort,

'It is the way the woman you love treats me.'

Then she thought that would be a vulgar thing to say and her father would disapprove.

Instead she replied,

"I don't – wish to – speak about it."

She looked away from the Earl as she spoke and therefore she did not realise that an understanding look had come into his eyes.

His lips had tightened, as if he was preventing himself from saying something that he might regret.

Then the butler was standing in the doorway and a footman opened the door of the carriage.

Sadira stepped out.

As she walked into the hall, there was the scent of beeswax and lavender.

It reminded her of how Langbourne Hall used to smell before her stepmother took over and she had swept away all the homemade bowls of pot-pourri and lavender.

They were replaced by exotic French perfumes that permeated the whole house.

"Her Ladyship's in the drawing room, my Lord," the butler informed him respectfully.

He led the way and opened a door.

Sadira saw at once that the room was furnished exactly as she had expected and again it reminded her of her own home before her stepmother had changed everything.

There was a comfortable sofa and armchairs round the fireplace and there were flowers everywhere that she was certain had not been bought in London but brought up from the Earl's garden in the country.

The Dowager Countess was seated in an armchair with a pretty lace antimacassar behind her head and a Chinese embroidered shawl covered her knees.

As the Earl advanced towards her, she held out both her hands in delight.

"Norwin, I am so thrilled to see you!" she exclaimed. "We were all so excited when I received your message saying that you would be dining here."

The Earl bent forwards to kiss his grandmother affectionately on both cheeks.

Sadira could see that she had once been very beautiful and her appearance was still striking with her white hair and a feminine elegance that was ageless.

She had several ropes of perfect pearls round her neck and she was wearing diamond earrings as well with pearl drops at the ends.

"I am delighted to see you, Grandmama," the Earl enthused, "and this is a very special occasion because I have brought Sadira Bourne with me."

"I wondered who would accompany you," his grandmother replied.

She held out her hand to Sadira and as she did so the Earl said,

"Sadira has promised to be my wife and I know, Grandmama, that you would want to be the first to hear of it."

The Dowager Countess gave a little cry.

"Your *wife*!" she almost shouted out. "Oh, Norwin, how wonderful! As you must have guessed, it is news that I have been hoping to hear for a very long time now."

She was holding Sadira's hand and did not let it go as she looked at her scrutinisingly and said,

"You are very lovely, my dear, and so like your mother, who was a good friend of mine for many years."

"You remember Mama?" Sadira asked.

"Very well indeed," the Dowager Countess replied, "and I can imagine nothing more perfect than that you should marry my charming grandson."

She looked up at the Earl and asked him,

"Why did you not warn me? I had no idea that after all these years of waiting you were contemplating becoming a married man."

"I did not contemplate it at all," the Earl admitted with a smile, "until I met Sadira."

"And she is everything you ever wanted," the Dowager Countess murmured quietly.

Because she was obviously so thrilled with the news, Sadira felt uncomfortably guilty at deceiving her and there was, however, nothing she could do but hope that she would never discover the truth.

The butler announced dinner and the Dowager Countess took her grandson's arm.

He then led her into the dining room while Sadira followed behind them.

The meal was what she had expected, good plain food but beautifully cooked.

Sadira was not surprised to hear that the cook had been with the Dowager Countess for nearly thirty years and she thought that the same might be true of the butler as well.

Also of the housekeeper whom she had encountered when she went up stairs after dinner to tidy herself.

It had been an unexpectedly interesting meal.

The Earl had exerted himself to tell his grandmother many things she wanted to know about what was happening on his estate in the country.

And there was a great deal of conversation about his horses, a subject that the Dowager Countess had a surprising good knowledge about.

Sadira found herself listening intently and enjoying the Earl's jokes and repartee.

After dinner the Dowager and Sadira returned to the drawing room and left the Earl to his decanter of port.

Now that they were alone, the Dowager Countess was bubbling over with excitement,

"I have never been so happy as I am tonight. I know, my dear, that you are exactly the wife I have always wanted Norwin to find."

"I hope I will – make him – happy," Sadira reacted to her a little uncomfortably.

"Of course you will," the Dowager answered, "and you will help him to forget how unhappy he was as a child."

Sadira must have looked surprised and the Dowager Countess explained,

"Norwin was only eleven when his mother died and I have never known a boy to be so upset and so unhappy. I did my best, as did our other relatives. But we had to leave him to be brought up by his father, who he never got on with and he was really miserable."

"Why should that have happened?" Sadira asked.

"I suppose that my husband, who was rather a strange character, was in a way jealous of Norwin."

The Dowager Countess paused and then added,

"I think a man can often be jealous of his own son because he will eventually take his place and also if his son is brilliant at sport, as he himself had always wanted to be."

"It seems rather odd," Sadira murmured.

"I agree," the Dowager Countess replied. "Yet it does happen and without his mother Norwin had a very difficult time with his father always finding fault with him and stopping him from doing anything he wanted to do."

The Dowager gave a deep sigh before she went on,

"This continued until, when he grew up, Norwin seldom went to Kensall Park, which we all regretted."

She put her hand on Sadira's arm as she paused and then resumed,

"I know, my dear, that you will try to make up for all he suffered as a boy and take him away from the fast heartless people who run after him because he is rich and powerful, but never attempt to understand him."

Sadira looked down at the floor as she felt that she could not meet the old lady's eyes.

Hers might tell her that she also did not understand the Earl and nor did she wish to.

"And now everything will be changed," the Dowager Countess went on as if she was speaking to herself, "and Norwin will have someone who loves him for himself rather than for his possessions."

Sadira knew that the Dowager Countess was thinking of the women like her stepmother who had pursued him.

And like the Marchioness, they would fight to keep the Earl's love even when he was married to her.

She could hardly tell his grandmother that she did not care what he did or who he spent his time with as long as it was not with her.

She only felt that the future was going to be more complicated that she had supposed and she so wished now that she did not have to pretend to this dear old lady that she loved her grandson.

She must never guess that it was quite impossible for her to make up for his unhappy childhood.

'I must not feel sorry for him,' she told herself.

It was then that the Earl came into the room.

"I have been to the kitchen, Grandmama," he said, "to tell Mrs. Field the good news. She is absolutely delighted and is determined to make my Wedding cake. But you know as well as I do that it will infuriate my own chef!"

His grandmother chuckled.

"Then you will just have to have a Wedding cake in every house you own," she said, "and two in London!"

Her eyes softened as she added,

"It's just like you, Norwin, to tell Mrs. Field. I know she must be really thrilled. She has been in a complete tizzy ever since you sent the message saying that you were coming to dine here."

"We will dine with you again next week," the Earl promised, "and then Sadira can meet all the old servants, as she will have to do in the country and naturally at Kensall House."

"The tenants and the whole village," the Dowager said, "will expect a special feast on your Wedding Day."

"They shall have fireworks and endless barrels of ale," the Earl promised.

He glanced at the clock and remarked,

"I know it is nearly your bedtime, Grandmama, so I am now going to take Sadira home."

"I think the truth is," his grandmother answered softly, "that you want to be alone. Take me up to bed and then you can stay here comfortably in front of the fire."

She gave a little laugh before she added,

"I remember years ago, when your grandfather was courting me, it was very difficult for us to get a moment alone to ourselves. There were always people round us, so sometimes we used to slip away from them and hide in the garden."

"Surely in your day that was considered most improper," the Earl teased her.

"Of course it was!" his grandmother answered. "Once we found a hiding place in the attic and I was in terrible trouble with my mother."

Her eyes twinkled as she carried on,

"But it was worth every moment of it."

The Earl offered her his arm.

"Let me take you upstairs, Grandmama," he suggested.

"You can take me to the foot of them," the Dowager answered. "My lady's maid will be waiting there. You remember she is Lucy, who used to be your nursery maid."

"Of course I have not forgotten Lucy," the Earl answered.

He escorted his grandmother from the room.

Before she left the Dowager Countess kissed Sadira affectionately on both her cheeks.

"You have made me very happy, dear child," she sighed. "One day, when you can spare the time, come and see me and I will tell how naughty and at the same time how adorable Norwin was when he was a little boy."

"I don't mind you doing that," the Earl said, "but leave Sadira to find out for herself how much I have blotted my copybook since then!"

He spoke jokingly, but, as Sadira met his eyes, she had a feeling that he was challenging her in some way.

When he and his grandmother had left the room, she stood gazing down into the fire.

She felt that if only this charade they were acting was real, how differently she would be feeling now.

She had always wanted to marry a man who had a keen knowledge of horses, who was athletic and strong and whose home was in the country.

It was one of the idyllic dreams that she had shared with Anne.

Now the background was perfect, but everything else was wrong.

The Earl was in love with a woman he could not marry and she knew that every moment they were together he was wishing that it was her stepmother who was beside him and not her.

As she thought of the Marchioness, she put her hand up to her cheek, which was still burning.

'How can I possibly – endure this sort of humiliation – happening to me not only now but every day in the future?' she asked herself.

She could envisage the years ahead as the Marchioness encroached more and more upon them and finally she herself would become nothing but a pale ghost.

She would move around the great house like a disembodied zombie where she was not wanted, unnoticed and totally alone.

When the Earl came back into the room, Sadira did not turn round.

He walked towards her and, when he reached her, he said,

"I can only say thank you for making my grandmother so happy."

"I dislike having to lie to anybody who is so kind and – who loves you so much," Sadira muttered in a low voice.

"I feel exactly the same," the Earl replied.

Sadira thought that he was then going to say something pertinent about the situation that both of them found themselves in.

Instead he said abruptly,

"Let me take you home, unless there is anywhere else you would rather go?"

"I would like – to go home," Sadira answered quietly.

She knew as she spoke that that this was untrue.

The Marchioness might be waiting for her and, if she could choose, she would rather be anywhere than under the same roof as her stepmother.

The carriage was waiting, the Earl assisted her into it and they drove back in silence.

Only as they neared Langbourne House did the Earl say,

"My Grandmother has suggested and, I think it is a good idea, that tomorrow we have luncheon with my aunt, Lady Winterton. She will invite a number of cousins and other relatives whom you will have to meet sooner or later."

Sadira did not speak and he went on,

"Our engagement will be announced in the newspapers tomorrow and it would be a mistake to give them cause to ask us why they had not been notified personally before its appearance."

He gazed at her before he went on,

"We can, in this way, prevent there being any complaints by meeting them before you go to any other parties."

"I understand," Sadira nodded. "At what time will you call for me?"

"At half-past twelve," the Earl replied, "and I feel sure that your father will understand if he is not invited to this luncheon."

Sadira knew what he was implying, it was that his aunt would not want her stepmother to be included in the invitation.

"I am sure that Papa already has several engagements arranged for tomorrow," Sadira said quickly.

The carriage duly arrived at Langbourne House and then the Earl jumped out to help her alight.

They went into the hall and, because the servants were listening, the Earl said,

"Goodnight, Sadira, and thank you again for what has been a very happy evening."

To her surprise he then took her hand and raised it to his lips.

She just knew that he was once again play-acting, but at the same time she had to admit that he played his part very gracefully.

As he left the house, she said to the butler,

"I would like you to know that his Lordship and I are engaged to be married. The announcement will be made in the newspapers tomorrow morning."

She saw the astonishment in the butler's eyes before he answered quickly,

"That's very good news, very good news indeed, my Lady, and, of course, I wish you and his Lordship every happiness."

"Thank you," Sadira replied.

She ran up to her bedroom, but did not ring for her maid and instead she undressed herself.

When she had put on her nightgown, she walked slowly across the room to the window and pulled back the curtains.

It was a clear night.

The stars were shining brightly and the moon was rising over the garden at the back of the house and turning the distant roofs to silver.

'What shall I – do?' Sadira asked the stars. 'How can I go on with this – farce?'

As she spoke, she felt as if her stepmother was there menacing her and preparing to strike her again.

'It's impossible – quite impossible,' she murmured.

Then suddenly, as if the stars were telling her what she should do, she had an idea.

It seemed unthinkable and yet she knew in her heart that it was a possible way out of the ghastly trap that she had been pushed so forcibly into.

It was going to be difficult, very difficult indeed.

Yet, because the stars had told her what she would do, she knew that it was feasible.

Just feasible if she was clever and resilient enough.

'Thank you – thank you,' she said to the stars deep in her heart.

She then closed the curtains and climbed slowly into bed, not to sleep but to think and to plan.

*

The next morning Sadira went riding early.

She stayed in Hyde Park for so long that, when she finally returned to the house, it was to learn that her stepmother had gone out.

She then changed her clothes, putting on one of her prettiest gowns and a most attractive bonnet.

The Earl called for her punctually, as she had anticipated at half past twelve.

Sadira recognised that he did not wish to come into the house and so she was waiting for him in the hall.

As soon as the carriage drove up, she was on the doorstep and therefore there was no reason for the Earl to alight or even approach the house

Today he had brought an open carriage and they drove off in the bright sunshine.

The coachman and footman on the box looked very smart and the two horses that drew them were perfectly matched and extremely well-bred.

It was easy to talk at length about them and the Earl's other horses and so avoid the subject of themselves.

His aunt's house was a large one and despite herself Sadira found that the Kensalls were all charming and delightful people.

They were obviously thrilled that the Earl was to be married and they went out of their way to let Sadira know how pleased they were that she was to be his bride.

Of course they never mentioned her stepmother, but she knew instinctively, however, that they were thinking that she had been a bad influence on the Earl.

They disliked his name being linked with hers in gossip, although they would have been far too circumspect to say so to his face.

So it was with genuine delight that they welcomed Sadira into the family.

What a pity that this is not true she found herself thinking, not once but dozens of times during the visit.

Every one of the Earl's relations wished to entertain her in their homes and, when at last they left, the Earl had half-a-dozen dates written down on a small pad that he carried in his pocket.

They climbed once again into the carriage and as they did so Sadira asked the Earl,

"Would it be possible on the way back to call in for only a few minutes at 29 Belgrave Square? There is something I particularly want to ask my friend, Anne Beecham."

"Yes, of course," the Earl agreed.

He told the footman that it was where they were to go first and they moved off into the sunshine.

"You were a huge success," the Earl praised her. "Every one of my relations acclaimed you as if you were an angel sent from Heaven!"

"They were – very kind," Sadira answered, "and I do so hate deceiving them – as I hated doing last night to your enchanting grandmother."

"Fortunately," the Earl replied, "they will never know that they have been deceived and they will therefore be your devoted admirers and, I hope, your friends for the rest of your life."

Sadira did not answer and he added,

"There are quite a number of my other relatives I want you to meet, but they live in the country and so I think that we should spend a few days at Kensall Park as soon as it can be arranged."

Sadira thought that this was another thing that would infuriate her stepmother.

The Earl must have known what she was thinking for he said quickly,

"I thought perhaps, as your father is so busy, I could ask one of my aunts to chaperone you so that there would be no need for him to leave London."

"That is a good idea," Sadira managed to reply.

They reached 29 Belgrave Square and she said a little hesitantly,

"I don't suppose – you want to – come in and so – as I shall be only a minute or two – it might be easier for you to – stay in the carriage."

"That is what I will do," the Earl replied.

Sadira alighted and the door of the house was opened by Watkins.

"Good afternoon, my Lady," he smiled.

"Good afternoon, Watkins. Is Miss Anne in?" Sadira asked.

"She's upstairs in her sitting room, my Lady. I expect you can find your own way."

"Yes, of course, Watkins," Sadira answered, "and is your rheumatism any better these days?"

The butler shook his head and she knew that it was the reason why he had no wish to climb the stairs unless he had to.

She ran up the stairs as fast as she could and burst in on Anne, who was writing at a desk by the window.

She jumped up with excitement in her eyes.

"Sadira!" she cried. "I had no idea you were coming to see me."

"I have only dropped in on my way home," Sadira answered. "I want to tell you that I think I have some money for Father Christopher."

"How splendid. I have not yet had the chance to ask Papa and I expect he will resent having to give money to me as well as Mama."

"Then you must try some of the people who have not yet already been approached," Sadira suggested. "But tell me, when is Father Christopher leaving? I thought he said that it is tomorrow."

"That is right," Anne replied, "and some of the people who were at Mama's meeting are going to see him off."

"Where is he leaving from?" Sadira enquired.

"From Tilbury and his cargo boat, which is called *The Idris*, is sailing at ten o'clock. I know this because I have just had to tell one of Mama's friends who is taking him some money, quite a lot, I believe."

"How splendid to have collected it so quickly," Sadira said, "and, if I get what I expect from Papa, I will see that he has it before he leaves."

"You are making me feel as if I have been very lazy, but I have really not had much time. I am writing out invitations now for Mama's next Charity, which is for people who are suffering terribly after a huge earthquake in Turkey."

"Your mother is wonderful!" Sadira enthused. "She is always helping somebody who is in dire need."

"I know," Anne replied, "but *I* have to write the invitations!"

Sadira kissed her friend.

"I would help you, but I must not keep the Earl waiting. He is in the carriage outside."

"I will peep at him out of the window. I saw the announcement of your engagement in the newspaper today and I do wish you every happiness, Sadira. I am going to save up to give you a really marvellous Wedding present."

"Thank you, thank you," Sadira answered. "Now I must go. I told the Earl that I would be only a minute."

Watkins bowed her out and she waved to him as they drove away.

"I suppose your friend, Anne, will be one of your bridesmaids?" the Earl remarked.

"She will be my Chief Bridesmaid," Sadira replied. "We have known each other since we were very small and she is my best friend."

"Those are the friends who really matter. One knows that whatever trouble one is in, they will always stand by and never let one down."

Sadira thought that this was what she had found herself.

She was sure that in the sophisticated Social world that the Earl moved in there would be few people who he could really rely on if she found herself in real trouble.

Real trouble – for instance being co-respondent in a divorce case with her stepmother!

They reached Langbourne House and, as the carriage came to a standstill, Sadira held out her hand.

"Thank you very much," she said to the Earl. "I enjoyed the luncheon and I think your relatives are all charming and undoubtedly very fond of you."

"That is what I think myself," the Earl answered, "and I am grateful to you for being so pleasant to them."

He did not take her hand, but climbed out of the carriage first in order to help her to the ground.

Sadira wondered if perhaps he would like to come into the house, but he said quickly,

"I doubt if your father is at home and I have a great deal of work to do. Perhaps you will give him my regards and say that I shall expect to see him at dinner tonight."

"Tonight?" Sadira questioned.

"There is a special dinner being given by the Secretary of State for Foreign Affairs," the Earl explained, "and I know that your father will be one of the guests."

"Yes, most certainly," Sadira replied, "they are great friends."

"I suppose," the Earl asked reflectively, as if he had just thought of it, "I could ask if I could bring you now that we are officially engaged."

"No, no, please," Sadira objected. "I have a great deal to do and actually I believe that I have had enough excitement for one day."

"Then we will meet tomorrow. I am sure that there will be a family luncheon of some sort and I will let you know as soon as it is arranged."

"Thank you," Sadira said, "and – goodbye."

She walked into the house and the Earl went back into the carriage.

As he drove away, he thought that for someone so young and inexperienced Sadira had come through a very difficult ordeal with flying colours.

He could imagine no one else he knew who could have carried it all off so splendidly.

First at the intimate dinner with his grandmother and then at the luncheon today, Sadira had not made a single mistake.

He was sure that there was no suspicion in anybody's mind that things were not as they appeared.

As he looked back, he realised that everything Sadira had said and done was exactly right.

Everyone in his family whom she had met so far were hysterical with delight about her.

He was thinking as he drove home that once again his luck had not failed him.

*

Inside the house Sadira found with relief that both her father and her stepmother were out.

She went up to her bedroom and locked the door.

She then went to the wardrobe room, which adjoined it, and picked up two large canvas bags.

They were what she had used at school. She had needed them when the girls were taken on expeditions involving a stay for one or two nights at the places they visited.

As the girls invariably had to carry their own luggage, they used canvas bags, which were lighter than leather cases would have been.

Now Sadira took from her wardrobe the plainest and simplest clothes that she possessed.

She packed them neatly and knew that it would be a mistake to be carrying anything surplus to essentials.

She therefore discarded a great many gowns, keeping strictly to what she deemed was absolutely necessary.

When the two canvas bags were packed, she replaced them in the wardrobe room, locked the door and took away the key.

By this time it was growing late in the afternoon.

But she knew that, if her father was at the House of Lords, he would not return until quite some time later.

Sadira then went into his bedroom.

Her father had a special safe there and, apart from him, only she knew the combination of the lock.

It was when her mother was ill and rather weak that she had been told how to open it and this was to enable her to put away her mother's jewellery as it was something that the maids were not allowed to do.

Sadira then locked the outer door to her father's bedroom so that his valet could not come in and interrupt her.

She went ahead and opened the safe and, as she had expected, she found a considerable amount of money inside it.

There was also some small change as he never left it lying about in drawers.

She went through the banknotes and took for herself what seemed to be a very large sum of money.

Equally she knew only too well that she would need it all at some stage..

She took some sovereigns and half-sovereigns, knowing that she herself possessed very little ready money.

Her father had always said that she could have what she wanted, but he thought it was a mistake for her to carry too much money around on her person and she therefore gave all her bills to his secretary for payment.

Now Sadira knew that she would have to look after herself.

She had to be practical and work out as near as she possibly could what she would need to last her for a long time.

Finally, when she had taken almost everything her father had in the safe, she locked it and then she went back to her own bedroom.

When her maid came in, she was writing letters at her secrétaire, which stood in a corner of the room near the window. She brought in the bath that Sadira would take before she dressed for dinner.

Having finished what she was writing, Sadira put the letters into envelopes and hid them underneath the blotter.

She remembered that her father and stepmother would be going out tonight to the same dinner as the Earl and so she would be alone.

She thought that she would have her meal brought up to her bedroom on a tray.

"I am tired," she said to the maid, "and I shall go to bed early, but now I am going to walk for a little while in the garden for a breath of fresh air."

"It be cooler now the sun's gone down, my Lady," the maid replied, "and I'll have your bath ready for you when you comes back."

"Thank you, Betsy," Sadira replied.

She went downstairs, not hurrying, and out through the French windows into the garden.

It was narrow, as were the gardens of the houses on either side of it, but it went back quite a long way to the Mews.

This was where her father and the owners of the neighbouring houses kept their horses and carriages.

She went out through the door at the end of the garden, leaving the lock on the latch.

As her father and stepmother were going out to dinner, the coachman and the footman would be on the carriage.

There would therefore be no one with the other horses in the stable and the doors to it were closed.

Sadira then walked down the Mews.

There was a groom whose Master was a very old man and her father knew him well, but he had been ill for some time.

His groom was usually to be found sitting outside his stable door or, having little to do, talking to other grooms.

When Sadira visited her father's horses, which she did frequently, he was often there and always greeted her politely.

She usually asked him how his Master was keeping and he would reply grimly,

"'Is Lordship ain't no better and me and 'is 'orses don't get enough exercise, but there ain't nothin' I can do about it."

Sadira had felt rather sorry for him.

Now she walked a little way down the Mews, where he was usually to be found and to her relief she saw him through the open door of one of the stables.

He was rubbing down one of the carriage horses and whistling to himself as he did so.

"Good afternoon, Britan," Sadira began.

"Afternoon, my Lady," he replied. "I sees in the newspaper this mornin' as you be goin' to be married and I 'opes you'll be ever so 'appy."

"Thank you, Britan," Sadira replied.

"And what a man you've chosen! 'Is 'orses be some of the best. I always 'as a bet on 'em when I 'as a chance and some money."

"Well, I only hope they will not disappoint you," Sadira replied.

There was silence for a moment and then she asked him,

"I wonder if you would do me a service?"

"I'll do what I can," Britan answered. "What be you askin' me to do, my Lady?"

"I want to go very early tomorrow morning to Tilbury Docks," Sadira replied, "but I am anxious that no one in my house should know what I am doing. Can I trust you to take me there and say nothing about it to anybody?"

"Cross me 'eart and 'ope to die!" Britan declared. "When I gives me word, I jolly well keeps it!"

"That is what I hoped you would say," Sadira sighed. "So I will tell you what I want you to do."

Britan stopped grooming the horse and came to stand beside her.

"What be your Ladyship up to?" he asked. "A bit of romance?"

"Perhaps that is what you would think it is, Britan, but as I told you, no one must know."

"I've given me word," he replied firmly.

"Then could you please be waiting here for me at six o'clock tomorrow morning?" Sadira asked.

Britan nodded and then she went on,

"I have two bags that I want to take with me. If I take them into the garden while the staff are having their supper, perhaps you could collect them without anybody being aware of it."

"Trust me, my Lady."

"I will put them just inside the garden door," Sadira stressed. "Here is the key."

She put it into his hand.

As he took it, he looked up and asked,

"Now, my Lady, what be you up to? You're not elopin', be you, 'cause if you are, you'll break 'is Lordship's 'eart."

"No, I am not doing that," Sadira said. "I need to go away for a short time, but I have been forbidden to do so. That is why I want your help, Britain."

She thought that he looked indecisive and she rapidly went on,

"I know I can trust you."

"'Course you can."

"If you know nothing and say nothing, then you cannot be held responsible for anything that happens to me," Sadira said, "so, please – please, once you have dropped me at Tilbury, forget all about it."

"I'll not do that," Britan answered, "but I won't say nothin' to nobody."

"I will certainly make it worth your while," Sadira said with a smile and adding,

"Six o'clock or perhaps I had better say a quarter to six as our coachman might be up early."

"Don't you fret," Britan said, "that lot don't strain themselves unless they 'as to."

"Very well then I will be with you at six o'clock sharp."

"I'll be waitin'," Britan promised, "and your bags'll be inside the carriage with you."

"Thank you – and I am very grateful," Sadira replied.

She hurried back into the house, having left the garden door locked behind her.

She had a nice hot bath and put on a pretty negligée.

What was brought up from the kitchen for her dinner was delicious, but Sadira was too excited to be hungry.

She was embarking on an exciting adventure.

It was not only the most outrageous thing that she had ever done but was also the most dangerous.

Yet the stars had shown her the way and she knew that somehow they would help and protect her.

When she was left alone, she took her bags downstairs and she knew that the servants would now be having their supper.

The senior servants ate in the housekeeper's room and the others were in the servants' hall.

And none of their windows faced onto the garden.

Wearing her nightgown and negligée, she went out through the French window onto the lawn.

It was growing dusk and she was sure that no one would notice her as she carried first one of the canvas bags and then the other down the garden to the door into the Mews.

She set them down by the door that she had given Britan the key to.

Then she went back as quietly as she could into the house.

In her room she took from beneath the blotter the two letters that she had written. One was to her father and one to the Earl.

To the Earl she attached with a clip a piece of paper on which she had written a note,

"*Please have this taken during the morning to the house of the Earl of Kensall.*"

She then went downstairs and put the envelope addressed to her father on his desk as she knew that he always went to his study immediately after breakfast.

Her stepmother would still not have been called as she was seldom woken before ten o'clock.

Sadira then went back to her bedroom.

'I am really sure that I have thought of everything,' she told herself.

Then, as if she was compelled to do so, she walked to the window and pulled back the curtains.

By now it was nearly dark and the first stars were beginning to twinkle in the sky.

She looked up at them.

'Show me the way,' she asked them. 'I know you will not fail me.'

Everything was very quiet.

She had the feeling that there was a sudden peace within herself and the fear and the horror had subsided.

'The stars will protect me,' Sadira whispered to the sky, 'I *know* they will.'

She climbed into her bed and fell asleep almost before her head had touched her pillow.

CHAPTER FIVE

The Earl awoke early and felt in need of some exercise.

He thought that only on horseback would he be able to shake off the depression that he had been suffering from for the last two days.

He went to the stables himself, selected one of his superb stallions and five minutes later he was riding towards Rotten Row.

He was mounted on the stallion that he had bought only a week before at Tattersalls salerooms before the bidding started for a large amount of sovereigns that he did not want to disclose to his friends and family.

He was feeling pleased to find that the stallion was very obstreperous and looking for a challenge.

It reared and bucked to show its independence and it took the Earl quite some time to get it under control.

There was nothing he enjoyed more than the age-old battle between man and beast and, when finally the stallion settled down to a steady trot, he recognised that he was the victor.

It was far too early in the morning for there to be any of the beautiful women who drove in their carriages down Rotten Row.

They invariably waved to him, expecting him to stop and talk to them so that they could flirt with him.

He was hoping, however, that he might see Sadira.

He knew that she rode early, but today there was no sign of her in Hyde Park.

He was thinking again about how tactful and charming she had been yesterday with all his relatives and in consequence he was not feeling as apprehensive about the future as he had been.

When he arrived back at Kensall House after his most satisfactory ride, he would have gone straight into the breakfast room.

Before he could do so, however, he was informed by the butler that there was a letter for him from Langbourne House.

This information swept the smile from the Earl's face and there was a distinct frown between his eyes as he walked over to the sideboard to choose what he would eat for his breakfast.

He was feeling certain that the letter in question came from the Marchioness.

He thought that it was both indiscreet and very tiresome that she should write to him at the moment.

He had already received one passionate letter, which he had read through quickly before he threw it into the fire.

This second one would undoubtedly say very much the same and so it would share the same fate.

'It is always the same,' he told himself angrily, 'a woman will never give up and wants a brief *affaire de coeur* to last forever.'

It was dangerous for her to write anything that the Marquis might see and also very stupid as well.

The knowledge of what was waiting for him spoilt his breakfast.

However, he refused to hurry and deliberately read both *The Times* and *The Morning Post* before finally he started to walk towards his study.

His secretary had arranged the usual pile of invitations for him and there was another pile of private and personal letters.

On his blotter was the letter that he could see was from Langbourne House.

He glanced at it and was at once aware that it was not addressed in the Marchioness's handwriting. Nor had she used her private writing paper, which was always rather vulgarly heavily scented.

This, he surmised, showed a little more sense and yet it made him angry that she should have written to him at all.

Therefore he put the letter to one side and began the task of wading through the pile of invitations.

He marked those he accepted with a tick and those he rejected with a cross.

And he then read his other personal letters, which his secretary had not opened.

Now he looked once again at the letter from Langbourne House.

He sighed deeply, picked it up and then opened it.

As he unfolded the piece of paper inside the envelope, he realised that it was not from the Marchioness but from Sadira.

Wondering why she should have written to him, he read,

"My Lord,

I have been thinking over our situation and I realise that, if I am suffering, so are you, only in your case it is worse.

I am aware that when we are together you are wishing that someone else was beside you and I think it would be impossible for us to go through life together in such circumstances day after day, week after week and month after month.

I have therefore decided to go away so that you will never see me again. I have told my father that I am going to Paris with some friends in order to buy my trousseau.

He will therefore not worry about me for at least two or three weeks and after that, when he cannot find me, he will have to accept that I am dead.

As our engagement has now been made public and I have been accepted by your family, 1 am quite certain that Papa will not do anything that would cause a scandal.

You are therefore safe and free and I can only wish you real happiness in the future.

There is one thing I would beg of you to do for me. My stepmother threatened, when I said that I had no wish to marry you, that she would have my horse, Swallow, taken away and starved to death and would give my dog, Bracken, to some man in the slums who would ill-treat him.

As I love both Swallow and Bracken more than anything else in the world, please, I beg of you, take care of them and don't let them suffer a horrible fate that they most surely do not deserve.

Sadira

The Earl sat back heavily in his chair as he could hardly believe that what Sadira had written about her horse and dog was true.

Yet he then remembered the red mark on her cheek and he was well aware that the Marchioness's emotions, whether of love or hatred, lacked all control.

But how could Sadira possibly go away, presumably abroad, and then just disappear?

He thought of how young and innocent of the world she was.

If she had gone away alone, as she appeared to have done, he could not bear to think of the trouble that she could find herself in.

She was so beautiful and, as he was well aware, every man who looked at her smiled and looked again.

He rose from his desk and walked across the room and, moving backwards and forwards, he tried to think of what he should now do.

He told himself that perhaps she had not gone away alone.

If she had told her father that she was going with friends to Paris, then she had probably left England with them.

The best thing he could do now was to try and prevent her from leaving her friends and going off on her own.

He ordered his carriage to be brought round to the front door and then went upstairs to change from his riding clothes.

When he had done so, he hurried down again, aware that it was now getting on for ten o'clock.

He drove rapidly to Langbourne House and asked the butler if he could see the Marquis at once.

To his relief he learned from the butler that he was in his study alone.

This meant, the Earl thought, that the Marchioness had not yet come downstairs and so there was no chance of him seeing her.

The butler opened the study door and announced him in an unnecessarily loud voice.

The Marquis, who was sitting at his desk, looked up in some surprise.

"Good morning, Norwin," he said.

"Good morning," the Earl answered. "I have called to see you because I have received a letter from Sadira."

The Marquis smiled.

"I thought she would write to you too. I have had a note from her saying that she has left for Paris. I suppose no young woman can resist buying her trousseau there."

"What she omitted to tell me," the Earl said, "is her address and, of course, I want to write to her."

"I can understand," the Marquis replied, "but you will hardly believe it, she has not told me who she is travelling with."

He turned over some of his papers.

"See for yourself," he said and handed Sadira's note to the Earl.

The Earl took it to the window and read it with his back to the Marquis.

To her father Sadira had written,

"Dearest Papa,

You left earlier last night than I expected and

*I did not have a chance to tell you that I have
been asked to go to Paris early tomorrow
morning with some friends of mine. I thought it a
marvellous opportunity to buy some beautiful
gowns for my trousseau, which I am afraid will
be somewhat expensive.*

*I know you will understand that I want to
look my best to please Norwin's family, who
have been so sweet and kind to me.*

*I have therefore taken some money from your
secret safe, which I hope you will not mind.*

Take good care of yourself, dearest Papa.

*You know that I love you and will miss you all the time
I am away.*

Goodbye.

Your loving daughter,

Sadira."

The Earl read the note through slowly and carefully and then once again.

It was just what he expected.

At the same time it was a blow since it gave him no more information than he had already which was virtually negligible.

He walked back to the desk.

"As you say," he remarked to the Marquis, "there is no address and I suppose you have no idea who these friends might be, my Lord?"

"I am afraid not," the Marquis answered. "It may be somewhat remiss of me, but in fact I have not met many of Sadira's friends since she left her Finishing School."

The Earl then thought that it would be a mistake to press him any further, so instead he suggested,

"Well, I am sure she will write to me as soon as she reaches Paris and, if you receive a letter in the meantime, perhaps you will let me know, my Lord."

"Of course I will," the Marquis promised.

"It is worrying that she should have been so foolish as not to leave more details, but I expect she was in a hurry to pack. I have learned from my butler that she had already left the house before her lady's maid called her."

The Earl thought this was no help either.

He then forced himself to talk briefly about other matters before he went back to his carriage, which was waiting outside.

As the horses were turning round, he had an idea.

Yesterday on the way home from the luncheon, Sadira had stopped to call on a friend in Belgrave Square,

She might well be one of the friends who she had left England with.

At least it was an idea that was worth exploring.

He therefore drove to 29 Belgrave Square and asked to see Miss Bourne.

He was shown by the butler into a sitting room on the ground floor and waited only a few minutes before Anne came in.

She had been informed by the butler who her caller was and the Earl could see by the expression on her face that she was surprised to see him alone.

Before he could introduce himself, she asked him,

"Is Sadira not with you, my Lord?"

"No," the Earl replied. "I have come to ask for your help because Sadira has left London and not given me the address of where she was going."

"Left London?" Anne exclaimed. "She said nothing about leaving when she came to see me here yesterday!"

"I think she has gone to the country," the Earl said, "but I have no idea if she is coming back tonight or tomorrow. I am arranging a luncheon party and I wish to be in touch with her immediately."

"Oh!" Anne answered him. "Then I expect she has gone to Langbourne Hall. If so, I am sure it is because she wants to see Swallow, her horse, and Bracken, her dog. Her stepmother will not let her take them with her in London and I know how greatly she misses both of them."

"Then I certainly hope she will be back this evening," the Earl said, "but I just wondered if she had said anything about her movements to you."

"No, she came to see me about Father Christopher," Anne replied.

She saw by the expression in the Earl's eyes that the name meant nothing to him and she explained,

"Father Christopher is a famous Medical Missionary whom Mama has been helping with his fundraising. He has been doing miraculous healing work in Africa, and is leaving today for Morocco. Both Sadira and I promised to collect some money to help him in his work."

"That is very kind of both of you and, of course, I would like to contribute."

Anne smiled.

"That is most generous, my Lord, but I thought it was your money that Sadira said she was taking to Father Christopher before he left."

"You say he is leaving today?" the Earl questioned.

Anne looked at the clock.

"He will have gone by now. Some of Mama's friends were seeing him off at Tilbury Docks. His ship was sailing at ten o'clock. I suppose that now Sadira and I will have to send the money we have collected for him on to Morocco."

"I am sure if you give it to the Moroccan Embassy it will reach him safely," the Earl commented.

"Mama can arrange all that," Anne answered lightly, "and please ask Sadira to come as soon as she can to tell me how much she has collected."

"I will and thank you for your help, Miss Beecham."

"I am afraid I have not been that helpful," Anne said, "but if you are giving a party tonight, I am sure that Sadira would not want to miss it."

The Earl said 'goodbye' to her and drove as fast as he could straight to Tilbury Docks. It took him some time because the traffic was heavy through the narrow streets of the City.

As soon as he arrived, he began questioning the Tilbury Docks Officials.

He learned that a cargo-ship, *The Idris*, had left Tilbury for Tangier punctually at ten o'clock that evening and aboard it had been the celebrated Medical Missionary known as 'Father Christopher'.

In addition the Earl asked if they had knowledge of the other passengers travelling on *The Idris* and all he could learn was that it was carrying a cargo of wood and was registered in Tangier.

The Captain was a Scotsman, but most of the crew were Arabs.

"There are not many English travellers aboard a cargo boat as a rule," one Official told him. "The cabins are often full with Africans wishing to live in England when they arrive here. But going back there's usually only a handful of people making the voyage which, as you might imagine, my Lord, is somewhat uncomfortable."

"That is rather what I expected," the Earl replied.

He was thinking about it all the way back to Kensall House.

He was convinced that Sadira had sailed that morning on *The Idris* and had somehow entailed herself onto this Father Christopher. There was no proof of it, but his instinct told him for certain that it was so.

And how was it possible for anyone who had always lived a life of luxury to tolerate the discomfort of a cargo ship?

Or indeed the sort of people who Sadira would encounter on such a journey?

He was well aware that men of Arab blood were greatly attracted to women with fair hair and white skins.

He found himself clenching his fists at the thought of what might happen to Sadira on such a hazardous voyage.

Then he remembered that Father Christopher was a Missionary and he could only hope and pray that he would look after her effectively.

*

Sadira reached Tilbury Docks as she had hoped a little before eight o'clock.

The roads were clear and the two excellent horses pulling the carriage made the journey in plenty of time.

When they arrived, Britan made enquiries as to which quay they would find *The Idris* moored to and they drove towards it.

Because it was still so early in the morning, Sadira saw with relief that there was no sign of Lady Beecham's friends.

There were only men stacking heavy planks of wood onto the deck of a large, dirty and dilapidated-looking cargo ship.

Britan called to a boy who was lounging about on the quayside to come and hold his horses.

Then he jumped down himself to open the carriage door for Sadira.

"Be this the ship you be a-sailin' on, my Lady?" he asked. "It don't seem the right place for a lady like you."

"It's going to Tangier," Sadira said, "and I only hope that they will have a cabin for me."

"Do you mean as you ain't booked one?" Britan enquired.

"No, I have not," Sadira admitted.

"Then you'd best let me do the talkin' for you," Britan suggested. "I don't trust them Arabs not to sting you. They don't understand that we don't bargain in this country."

Sadira suddenly felt helpless.

It was one thing to think that she could run away and disappear forever with Father Christopher. It was quite another to be confronted with what was very far from her idea of a passenger ship.

It had never struck her that the crew would be Arabs. She could see them working and she knew that they had little respect for women.

There was every chance now that, having come as far as this, she might have to go home again.

On an impulse she turned to Britan,

"Please – help me! I am travelling with a Missionary called   Father Christopher. He is not here yet – and actually he does not – know that I am – going with him."

Britan stared at her in surprise.

Then he said,

"I suppose you knows what you're a-doin', my Lady, but it just don't sound right to me!"

"Please – don't keep calling me 'my Lady'," Sadira said quickly. "I have been thinking as we came here that I would call myself by my own name, but without my title and spelling it differently. You understand that I don't want anybody to be able to trace me here."

"I thinks as 'ow you be runnin' away," Britan answered, "and I only 'opes it's with some nice gentleman as'll look after you."

"No, Britan, I am going on my own," Sadira stressed firmly. "I have – to go so please – please help me."

She sounded so pathetic and so Britan stopped arguing and lifted her canvas bags out of the carriage.

He put them down on the ground and then said to the small boy who was standing by the horses,

"Now you keep 'old of them 'orses for me and see they don't move. I'll pay you for your pains when I comes back."

"I'll take extra good care of them," the boy promised. "I likes 'orses."

He was patting both of them as he spoke.

As if Britan sensed that he could trust him, he walked off without saying anything more to him.

Carrying Sadira's bags, he climbed up the gangplank.

Sadira followed him as he pushed through a door that led to the ship's accommodation.

There was a room with a dirty glass window that Sadira knew on a larger vessel would indicate the Purser's Office.

Britan walked up to it. There was no sign of anyone and he knocked on the door with his fist, asking loudly,

"Be there anyone at 'ome 'ere?"

An unshaven man who was obviously an Arab appeared from the back to say in broken English,

"Captain on bridge. What you want?"

"I wants a cabin for this lady," Britan replied, "and it 'ad better be a good 'un."

The Arab found a torn piece of paper and on it was marked a number of squares, which obviously represented the cabins of the cargo ship.

Some had a cross on them, which told Sadira that they were already engaged.

The Arab was looking for a pen and she whispered to Britan,

"Ask where Father Christopher is sleeping."

He nodded and, when the Arab came back, he asked him,

"This lady's workin' with Father Christopher and wants to be next to him. Where's 'is cabin then?"

The Arab pointed with his finger to a square that appeared to be on the upper deck.

"Then the lady'll 'ave the one next to 'im." Britan persisted.

"That cabin for two," the Arab replied.

Britan was about to ask for a single cabin when Sadira said to him again in a whisper,

"I will pay for a double cabin if it means I can have one to myself."

It was then the bargaining began.

The Arab clearly understood English better than he could speak it. He answered in monosyllables and yet he was very sure of what he wanted.

Sadira could see that Britan had been right in his assumption that the man would ask far more than he expected finally to receive.

At last, after much haggling and waving of arms, they came to a compromise.

Sadira produced the money, which the Arab grabbed quickly.

It told her that, although Britan had beaten him down, she was still paying more than the going rate.

The Arab came out of the Office and took them along a narrow passage and Sadira was beginning to be apprehensive of what she might be confronted with.

To her relief, however, when the cabin door was opened it was small but clean. It was not an inside cabin and had a porthole so she could see the sea.

The two bunks took up most of the room with only a very narrow space between them.

She was just about to say that she was content with the cabin when Britan exclaimed,

"There be nothin' on them beds! What about blankets?"

The Arab grinned.

"You pay," he snapped.

And once again they were haggling.

But before they had gone very far, Britan insisted that he should see the blankets.

The Arab went from the cabin and beckoned.

"You stay 'ere," Britan said to Sadira, "and leave this to me."

He went away and Sadira sat down on one of the bunks.

She thought how foolish she had been as she should have noticed that, while both bunks had coarse straw mattresses on them, there were no pillows or blankets.

Nor were there any rugs on the rough wooden floor.

She sat stiffly on one of the bunks and waited for Britan and the Arab to return.

There was the spasmodic sound of the men stacking wood in the hold and shouting to each other as they did so.

Suddenly she began to feel frightened.

Was she really brave enough, she now asked herself, to carry out her plan and leave England never to return?

Would it not be better to marry the Earl?

Then she thought of her stepmother and that anything would be better than being aware of the hatred that vibrated towards her every time she saw her stepmother.

It would be preferable even to be alone and defenceless in an Arab City or to have to sleep on a filthy bed infested with vermin.

She was deep in her thoughts when Britan and the Arab returned to the cabin only a short time later.

He was smiling and carrying two blankets while the Arab held two others in his arms and they seemed to be reasonably clean and presentable.

The Arab threw them down on one of the bunks.

Sadira held out some money towards Britan and he took it from her and then passed it on to the Arab.

It must have been to his satisfaction, because he beamed and even made Sadira a slight *salaam* before he left the cabin.

"Thank you for doing all that for me, I could not have handled myself," Sadira said to Britan. "It was clever of you to notice that there were no blankets on the bunks."

"They ain't got no sheets, but them blankets be new and well washed. Some of what 'e showed me I wouldn't let a dog sleep on!"

"I am very grateful," Sadira sighed.

"They didn't 'ave no pillows either," Britan went on, "so I got you an extra blanket as you can roll up and put under your 'ead. You'll be quite comfortable like that."

"I am sure I shall be," Sadira replied. "And thank you, thank you very much again. I could not have – done it without – you."

She then pressed some money into his hand. She had doubled what she had originally intended to give him before they started out.

He thanked her and turned towards the door.

"You take good care of yourself," he advised, "and if things don't work out, come 'ome. I never did trust these 'ere foreigners! And I wouldn't trust this lot any further than I could throw 'em!"

"I will be – all right," Sadira answered, "and thank you once again."

She held out her hand and Britan shook it.

"God bless you, my Lady, and, if you asks me, you'll really need Him lookin' after you on this 'ere trip of yours."

When he had gone, Sadira closed the cabin door.

She went over to the porthole hoping that she would be able to see the quay and she found that she could see at least part of it.

Since she had come on board she realised that quite a number of other people had now arrived.

Sadira was not certain whether they were passengers or seamen getting the ship ready for the voyage.

She, however, could see Britan driving away and she waved rather wistfully after him.

As he did so, she felt that she was losing her last contact with the civilised world she knew.

She opened the porthole wider to let in some fresh air and by standing on tiptoe and poking her head out she had a better view of the quay than she had before.

Now she could just glimpse the gangway that she had aboard on and she recognised that it was to be used only by the passengers.

There was another gangway further along the ship's side for those working on board.

Time went by and then she was aware that carriages were arriving and she was sure that some of them would contain Lady Beecham's friends.

They had doubtless come to see Father Christopher off and give him what money they had already collected for him

It was a considerable relief to her when she was certain that he was aboard the cargo ship.

She had a sudden fear that, despite the fact that his cabin was booked, he might change his plans at the last moment in which case she knew that she would be too frightened to go on alone.

Another carriage then arrived at the quay and now she could see Father Christopher getting out of it.

He was accompanied by another man who was wearing a cassock.

He did not look as if he was a traveller and Sadira thought that he must be another Missionary seeing Father Christopher off.

As soon as Father Christopher appeared, the ladies waiting for him climbed out of their carriages.

They clustered around him and Sadira could see that they were all giving him small parcels and envelopes.

Then she was aware that two of the ladies carried wicker baskets on their arms and it struck her that perhaps she should have brought some food with her.

She thought that it was very foolish of her not to think of it before, but her mind had been so cluttered with all her plans.

Finally, after a great deal of conversation, Father Christopher started to climb up the gangway.

He had said 'goodbye' to most of the ladies and then two who were laden with his gifts climbed up the gangplank after him.

Now Sadira could not see him, but a few minutes later she heard his deep voice and the high-pitched chattering of the ladies' voices.

They were in the cabin next to hers and she could hear quite clearly what they were all saying and so she realised that there was only a thin partition between them.

"I hope we have thought of everything that you will need, Father," one of the ladies remarked.

"You have been more than kind," Father Christopher replied, "and I am very grateful indeed for all you have given me, especially the money, which will be used for those who most need it in Morocco."

"We shall all be thinking of you, Father, and collecting more money, which we will send to you through the British Embassy."

"God will bless you for your generosity," Father Christopher sighed.

There was more chatter and then Sadira heard a voice calling out,

"All ashore! All ashore!"

"We must go," one of the ladies cried. "Goodbye, dear Father, and remember us in your prayers."

"You may be quite certain that I will," Father Christopher promised.

He said 'goodbye' a dozen more times before Sadira heard the ladies hurrying away and she thought that Father Christopher had followed them.

She heard the engines start up and a few minutes later the cargo ship began to move.

Looking out of the porthole, Sadira could see the ladies waving their handkerchiefs and she guessed that Father Christopher would be waving back to them from the deck.

The ship increased its speed and the quay was now out of sight and Sadira went back to sit on the side of one of the bunks.

Now that she was actually leaving England, she was feeling really frightened.

Suppose Father Christopher refused to take her and put her ashore before they reached the open sea. She was not at all certain how he could do it, but it was certainly a possibility in her mind.

So she decided that it would be wise not to reveal her presence until it was impossible for him to send her home.

She then heard him go into his cabin and close the door behind him.

She made up her bunk with the clean unused blankets that Britan had so cleverly found for her and she took off her jacket and hung the cape that she had brought with her on a hook on the wall.

Although it was hot at the moment, she thought that perhaps when they reached the Bay of Biscay it might be cold.

She had therefore brought a travelling cape with her that had belonged to her mother and was lined with fur.

She had packed only her plainest clothes, but the cape was an exception as she thought that it would be a mistake to shiver.

The ship had now reached the Straits of Dover and was beginning to pitch a little.

Sadira lay down on her bunk and she put her head, as Britan had suggested, on a rolled-up blanket and to her surprise it was really quite comfortable.

She decided to wait for at least an hour before she went to see Father Christopher and she was actually rather intimidated at doing so.

He might be angry with her and he might, when they reached Tangier, insist on sending her back on the next ship going to England.

Then she remembered that he had no jurisdiction over her and what was more she had the money that she had taken from her father's safe.

'I must be very careful that it is not stolen from me,' she thought and then trembled a little.

It was no use, she ruminated in pretending even to herself that everything did not depend on Father Christopher.

She had met him only once, but now she was asking him to take her under his protection.

'Please – please, God, make him look – after me,' she prayed fervently.

CHAPTER SIX

Sadira was tired by the time they reached Fez, which was not surprising.

She expected to have a quiet time on *The Idris* as long as Father Christopher accepted her as being there.

He had been, when she first approached him, very surprised.

But he accepted without argument her decision to leave home and Sadira thought that it was wonderful of him, especially when he said,

"You have come as my student and that is what you must be. If you have to look after yourself, you will be safer with Missionaries like me and working with them."

"That is exactly what I want," Sadira answered, "and thank you, Father, thank you for being so understanding."

"I don't say that I approve," Father Christopher replied, "but we all have to live our own lives and, if it is God's will, then you will succeed in all that you have undertaken."

As his student, Sadira was astonished to find how much there was to do.

Father Christopher was the only one with any medical knowledge aboard the ship and he was busy, Sadira found, from first thing in the morning until last thing at night.

The men who had carried the heavy cargo of wood on board the ship had injured their hands, their shoulders and their feet. And they all asked for treatment from the good Father.

Then, before they had sailed very far into the Bay of Biscay, there was a violent storm with endless lightning and deafening thunder.

One seaman broke an arm, another his leg and there were many with painful bruising from the violent rocking of the ship.

Father Christopher tended them all very skilfully and patiently.

Sadira had to help him with bandaging and the plaster, which fortunately he had brought with him.

In fact one large trunk was filled to the brim with nothing but medical supplies, which Father Christopher was taking to Fez and quite a lot of these had to be used on the voyage.

By the time they sailed into the Port of Tangier, Sadira was priding herself on becoming quite expert at nursing.

Father Christopher was eager to reach Fez as quickly as possible to discover why they needed him so much.

He therefore hired horses rather than mules and they set off from Tangier with a caravan of Arabs to assist them and indeed protect them on the long journey South.

The horses carried small tents that Sadira and Father Christopher could sleep in at night and it fascinated her how quickly the tents could be erected and dismantled by a coordinated team.

The countryside that they were passing through was not of any particular interest and she was glad that they did not have to stay in any of the small towns and villages that they passed through.

The ground at first was parched and cracked.

A few hawks swayed lazily in the sky and once or twice they disturbed a brilliantly coloured goldfinch.

Then they rode over marshy plains and later past a few forests of cork trees.

It took them all of eight days to reach Fez.

Before they arrived in the City, Father Christopher told Sadira that it had been built in about A.D. 800 and so was very ancient.

"Fez the devout," he said, "is one of the most revered religious centres of the Muslim world, but it is not now as powerful as it had been in the past. Today far too many people live there. In fact there are nearly two hundred thousand inhabitants in the Old City alone."

Sadira did not envisage quite what that really meant until they reached the City of Fez.

Late in the evening they descended the steep, narrow and sunless passages that were not really worthy of being called streets.

They passed the Quarawiyin Mosque, which she was told could accommodate twenty-two thousand worshippers but only Muslims were admitted.

Then, at last, when it was almost too dark to see the way, they stopped in a tiny square.

The houses around the square looked rough and in desperate need of repair.

Sadira could not believe that they were going to stay there, but then Father Christopher informed her with a sigh of satisfaction,

"We have arrived!"

As he spoke, the door of one house opened and a stream of people came running out.

They were waving their hands in welcome and talking at the tops of their voices.

During the voyage in *The Idris* Sadira had learned a little Arabic both from Father Christopher and from his patients.

She was suddenly aware that the people were all thanking God that he had reached them safely and she felt that they were clearly expecting him to solve all their problems whatever they might be.

They had ridden all day with hardly a stop for anything to eat and, as Sadira dismounted, she thought that the only thing she really needed at this stage was a bed to sleep in.

She had, however, first to partake of a large meal that had been specially prepared for Father Christopher.

The people had been making ready for him for whatever day he arrived and they never stopped talking for a single moment.

She learned later that they were all Christians and it was because they were having a difficult time with the local Muslims that they were so eager for Father Christopher to join them.

The house, built mostly of wood, was very primitive and, as she might have expected, they all sat on the floor with the food spread out in front of them.

The main dish was *couscous*, made with a kind of semolina and topped with a savoury stew, which was surprisingly palatable.

Sadira also liked the almond and honey cakes that were always served, she learned, at a meal in Morocco.

She had, since arriving at Tangier, become accustomed to eating with her fingers and she was told that the Moroccans believed that to use cutlery of any sort was a very dirty way of eating.

After the meal was over, she was able to climb up the rickety staircase and she was shown into a small rather airless room where there was a divan raised about six inches from the floor. And there was a deep and comfortable mattress lying on top of it.

She was feeling far too tired to take anything out of her bags except for her nightgown.

Her last thought before she lay down was that in this strange rabbit-warren-like City there would be a great number of injured or sick people.

They would all be in need of Father Christopher's skills and tomorrow and all the days that followed were likely to be very busy and hectic.

Below Father Christopher was being plied with questions as to why he had brought an English girl with him.

"She is my disciple," he stipulated firmly and refused to add any further information.

*

Outside the Old City of Fez in the impressive and luxurious Palace of the Sultan, the Earl had been waiting impatiently for nearly a week.

When he left Tilbury, he was convinced that he knew where Sadira had gone.

He had returned to Kensall House in his carriage and there he sent for his secretary, Mr. Barrett.

He informed him that he was leaving England at once in his yacht, which was at that time anchored in Dover Harbour.

Mr. Barrett was appalled.

"But how can you do so, my Lord?" he asked. "You have a great number of important engagements, two with His Royal Highness and the Prime Minister is expecting you at a Conference he is holding on Thursday."

He paused and then continued,

"And there are also the parties that you have arranged for your relatives to meet Lady Sadira."

"I know that, Barrett," the Earl agreed, "and you will somehow have to cover up for me."

He paused as if in deep thought and then continued,

"Tell His Royal Highness and the Prime Minister that I am visiting a relative who is dying and then inform my relatives that the Prime Minister has sent me abroad on an urgent mission."

He paused again and then resumed,

"In fact I am leaving for Morocco as soon as I can reach *The Mermaid*."

This was the name of the Earl's yacht and it was always expected to be in readiness for him to leave England at short notice.

He had, however, not used *The Mermaid* for at least three months and Mr. Barrett was told to send a warning to the Captain of his Master's imminent arrival at Dover.

He was also given the task of saving Sadira's horse, Swallow, and her dog, Bracken.

The Earl told him to arrange for Swallow to be removed from the stables of Langbourne Hall together with Bracken and have them taken at once to Kensall Park.

Leaving Mr. Barrett gasping with the number of his orders, he ran upstairs to supervise his packing.

Hopkins, his valet, was used to his Master making quick decisions and then expecting them to be carried out at the double.

He had been an excellent Batman to the Earl in the Army and this had taught him how to cope with any emergency with considerable dexterity.

His duties had involved a good deal of travelling on the Continent and in other parts of the world.

And now he was delighted at the opportunity of getting away from the humdrum routine in England.

Even by the Earl's standards it seemed as if his luggage was packed and ready with the wave of a magic wand and he drove off in his four-in-hand towards the coast with Hopkins sitting behind him.

All of this was thanks to Mr. Barrett's efficient organisation in anticipating the Earl's requirements even before he had thought of them himself.

The Mermaid had been alerted in good time and the yacht moved out of Dover Harbour the minute the Earl stepped aboard.

As he shortly went up onto the bridge to be with the Captain, the Earl felt glad to be leaving London behind.

For the moment he would be no longer be worried by the problems created by the Marchioness and, of course, there would be the Marquis's distress when he could not find Sadira.

'How can she have thought of anything so outrageous as disappearing completely!' the Earl asked himself.

At the same time he could not help admiring her courage in taking the initiative and he could easily understand her violent revulsion against a situation that was clearly so abhorrent to her.

He knew, if he was honest, that it was the sort of thing that he would have done himself.

It seemed extraordinary, however, that one small, rather fragile-looking girl could run away.

Could she really believe that she could live her life on her own without anybody trying to find her?

'It's a crazy idea!' the Earl said to himself scornfully and yet he could not help thinking that it was a very brave one.

The Bay of Biscay proved to be just as uncomfortable for *The Mermaid* as it had been for *The Idris*.

Sadira had not been seasick and, as there had been so many casualties, she had been too busy to think about herself.

Just the same happened on *The Mermaid*.

Three seamen were injured during a vicious storm and the Earl took the Captain's place on the bridge while he attended to them.

He was not as skilful as Father Christopher, but the three of them were hobbling about a few days later.

Having learnt from the Officials at Tilbury that *The Idris* was going to Tangier, the Earl decided to put into the Port of Rabat on the Atlantic coast of Morocco.

It was a little nearer to Fez than the other alternative Ports and it took him only six days to reach the outskirts of the City.

He was fortunate in finding two good horses for himself and his valet from a local horse dealer, but his luggage had to be carried by mules and this caused them to slow down more than he would have wished.

However, when he finally arrived in Fez, he went straight to the Sultan's Palace.

He had stayed with the Sultan on a previous visit some four years earlier and he had also entertained the Sultan when he visited London.

He therefore knew that he would be welcome and he had instructed Mr. Barrett to advise the Moroccan Embassy in London of his intention and to be in touch with the Sultan.

He learnt on arrival that they had sent a Courier overland to inform the Sultan of his imminent arrival.

The Earl was received at The Palace with great delight and the Sultan, who was a comparatively young man, immediately started to talk to him about his horses.

It was such a familiar conversation that it scemcd as if thcy had picked it up just where they had left off four years ago.

So it was quite a while before the Earl was able to explain why he had come to Fez.

He told the Sultan that he wished to get in touch urgently with the Missionary, Father Christopher.

The Sultan immediately gave instructions that the Earl was to be told as soon as Father Christopher was known to have arrived in Fez.

And the Earl realised that it might well be a number of days before this happened and therefore he relaxed and enjoyed himself.

The Sultan was very intelligent and had surrounded himself with some of the best brains in Morocco.

The lengthy luncheons and dinners he gave for the Earl were attended, of course, entirely by men and there was no question of any of the women in the Sultan's *harem* eating with them.

It was very hot in the daytime, but refreshingly cool at night.

There were a number of interesting sights in Fez that the Earl had not seen on his last visit.

The days passed, but when there was no news of Father Christopher, the Earl began to grow impatient.

He wondered if, after all, the Missionary had not made his way straight to Fez and he might instead have chosen to linger in some other town.

There were one or two on the route that, as the Earl knew, would welcome a Medical Missionary.

The day after Sadira had arrived the Earl and the Sultan had gone to a camel market.

It had taken place some way outside the City and it had proved very interesting to watch the camels being paraded round a ring and then being sold to the highest bidder.

There were also a number of horses for sale that the Earl inspected carefully and he advised the Sultan which ones were the best in his opinion.

They were late arriving back at The Palace and the Earl climbed up two storeys to his room to change for dinner.

He thought as he did so that he was growing bored with eating *shish kebab* and deep-baked chicken *tajine*. Also a steaming mountain of *couscous*, which was prepared in Fez and contained cinnamon and sweet yellow raisins.

He felt irritated by the small plates of peppery condiments, olives, nuts, and sweetmeats that were frequently offered to him by the Sultan's most attentive servants.

What he really wanted was a glass of champagne rather than the scalding and intensely sweet green mint tea.

Nevertheless he knew that all this was what would be waiting for him when he went down the stairs and he recognised that what was really upsetting him was the fact that he had not yet found Sadira.

He finished his meal with the Sultan with some relief.

As he did so, one of the servants, first making an obeisance, informed him that Father Christopher had arrived the previous evening.

"Why was his Lordship not informed immediately?" the Sultan demanded angrily.

The man explained with embarrassment that they had been watching the main entrance into the

City and Father Christopher, he claimed, had entered by a less well used gateway.

The Sultan was extremely annoyed that his orders had not been carried out efficiently enough.

The Earl, however, was greatly comforted and he thanked him for a delicious meal and asked if he could have a guide.

He wished to be taken immediately to wherever Father Christopher was staying.

The moon was shining brightly as he left The Palace so that it was easy to see the way to the entrance of the Old City.

Then they were walking through the endless narrow passages where the moon could not percolate and it was very dark and somewhat foreboding.

Although it was growing late, the passages were crowded with people.

There were children carrying wooden trays of bread dough on their heads, women doing the family wash at an exquisitely tiled public fountain and bearded old men selling caged birds.

The old Berber women with tattooed chins squatted on the kerbs with their hands held out as they begged for money from the passers-by.

There were numbers of ragged porters dragging or pushing slow-moving donkeys loaded down with sheepskins.

The Earl followed behind his guide closely, who was wearing the traditional long white *djellaba* with its sharply peaked hood like all the other men in the streets.

The night air was clamorous with rhythmic hammerings as the iron workers were busy on their kettles and there were coppersmiths tap-tapping on ornate trays and the continual sound of the high voices of street vendors.

The guide twisted in and out of the passages, apparently well aware of where he was going.

They were moving swiftly and, as they went deeper and deeper into the Old City, they were continually interrupted by the cry,

"*Balek! Balek!*"

The Earl knew already from his previous visit to Morocco that this meant, 'make way'.

He moved quickly into a doorway as a donkey came round the corner and it as usual carried so much on its back, whatever the load, that it swept against the Earl's chest as it passed by him.

Then the guide was now off again and they were moving through an aroma of spices and newly-cut cedar wood, singed ox-horn and hot cooking oil.

The Earl began to think that they must have reached the very bottom of the hill where the City of Fez was first built.

There was suddenly a flaring light ahead of them and the guide turned his head to say to the Earl,

"Fire, Excellency. House on fire!"

The Earl knew that this often happened in Fez for the majority of the houses in the Old City were built of wood.

They walked on and now the Earl saw in front of him that there was a small square with a fountain in the centre of it.

On the far side of the square a crowd had collected to stare at one of the houses and out of its doors and windows flames were leaping up into the sky.

The guide kept going forward towards it and the Earl followed him.

As they drew nearer still, he was suddenly afraid that this might just be the house where Sadira was staying.

Even as he thought of it, he saw a white-haired man who was taller than the crowd around him.

He was wearing a cassock and the Earl then struggled to reach him, but the crowd was too thick.

As he moved forward a little, he saw several women being brought out through the door of the burning house.

As one of them was supported outside by two men, she screamed,

"My baby! My baby! It is left behind. *My baby!*"

Her voice rose to a shrill screech.

And then from the other side of the man with the white hair the Earl amazingly saw Sadira move forward to speak to the woman.

Then Sadira ran straight into the house that the people had just escaped from.

He could hardly believe his eyes as he watched what was happening.

There was a murmur among the crowd, as if they were protesting at what Sadira had just done.

The Earl suddenly realised that he was just standing there staring at the flaming house.

Quickly he pulled off his coat and said to his guide urgently,

"Give me your *djellaba.*"

The guide took it off and thrust it into the Earl's arms.

Moving to the fountain, he dipped the *djellaba* into the water.

When it was fully soaked, he lifted it out dripping with water and put it on.

"Now I want another one," he ordered sharply.

This the guide translated into Arabic and a man standing near the Earl understood what he wanted

He pulled off the *djellaba* that he was wearing and then thrust it into the fountain.

The Earl snatched it from him and, as the people moved rapidly to one side, he ran into the burning building after Sadira.

Inside the centre of the house was not burning as violently as the outer walls.

There was a staircase in front of him and he was about to climb it, thinking that the baby Sadira had gone to rescue would be on the first floor.

There was a sudden crash and the staircase to the front of him collapsed in flames and smoke.

It was then, as the Earl stared in dismay, that he saw Sadira.

She had come from a back room behind the staircase and, as the staircase was torn apart, she stopped and looked upwards.

The Earl knew at once that she was praying.

Then the leaping flames seemed suddenly to encircle her, enveloping her in a halo of light.

Just for a second the Earl looked at her with the baby held close to her heart.

Then he ran forward and without speaking threw the soaking *djellaba* over her, covering her head with the hood.

He lifted her and the baby up into his arms.

"Hide your face against me!" he urged Sadira.

As he felt her obey him, he moved towards the door.

By now the fire had complete control of the house and the Earl knew that the only thing he could do would be to rush his way through the flames.

Holding Sadira very tightly in his arms, he bent his head and took a deep breath.

Then he crashed through the fire and out into the cool darkness beyond.

As he did so, the crowd started cheering.

When he reached them, a dozen hands beat out the flames which, despite the wetness of the *djellaba*, had started to burn the cotton at its edges.

Aware that he was outside and still alive, the Earl pushed back the hood from over his head.

Gently he removed the *djellaba* covering Sadira that had concealed the baby from the crowd.

When they saw that he had brilliantly rescued them both, they cheered even more loudly.

The mother of the child went down on her knees before the Earl.

She kissed his feet before she rose to take the baby from Sadira's arms with streams of tears running down her cheeks.

"He is – all right. He is – not hurt," Sadira stammered in a trembling voice that seemed to come from a long distance away.

As if to confirm her words, the baby started to cry.

The Earl threw off his smoking *djellaba* and once again picked Sadira up in his arms.

"I will take you home," he promised gently.

She was too overcome and shocked by what had happened to be able to reply.

She just closed her eyes and rested her head against his shoulder.

Father Christopher then came to the Earl's side.

"I can only thank God," he said, "that you were here and that your bravery has saved Sadira when I thought it impossible for her to survive the intense heat of the fire."

"I am taking her now to The Palace," the Earl replied, "and I would like to see you in the morning please."

"Of course," Father Christopher nodded.

With Sadira in his arms the Earl followed the guide who was leading them back through the Old City.

The crowd made way for them to pass and get away from the now smouldering house.

And once again they were in the narrow darkened passages, but this time moving uphill instead of down.

It was a long way back to The Palace, but the Earl found that Sadira was very light.

Far too light and too fragile, he reflected, to have even attempted such an amazing act of courage.

He knew that, if he had not been there, she would most certainly have been burned to death.

After some time they reached the gateway of the Old City.

Now it was easy to see by the light of the moon and Sadira stuttered,

"I-I think I can – walk now."

'There is no need for you to do so," the Earl answered, "and the sooner you can rest after all that you have been through the better."

"H-how could – you be there, how could you – suddenly appear – when I thought – both the baby and I must – d-die?"

"I will tell you about it tomorrow," the Earl replied. "Now you are going to be the guest of the Sultan and I think you will find it very much more comfortable than where you have been staying."

She looked up at him in surprise and the light of the moon was full on her face.

The Earl thought that no woman could be more beautiful and at the same time somehow pathetic and in need of protection.

He did not say anything more as he walked through The Palace garden and into the great building itself.

The guide had gone ahead of them, talking in his own language to explain to the Sultan's servants what had happened in the Old City.

One of them, obviously with some authority, led the way for them upstairs.

The Earl carried Sadira into what he knew was one of the best guest rooms. There was a luxurious divan to sleep on and cushions to sit down on were set out on an exquisitely made carpet.

Very gently he put Sadira down on the bed.

She was wearing, he could see, only a simple muslin gown which he was aware would have burnt quickly if the flames had caught it.

She looked up at him from the bed.

Her face was very pale, but there was a smile on her lips.

For a moment they were alone in the room while the manservant went to fetch maids to attend to Sadira.

"Is it – really really true that you are – h-here and – and you have – saved me?" Sadira whispered.

"It is true," the Earl answered.

As he spoke, he bent forward and kissed her gently on the lips.

Then, the maids came hurrying into the room, chattering loudly at the horror of what had happened in the Old City.

The Earl straightened himself and moved away from the bed.

Just for a second his eyes met Sadira's.

Then, knowing that there was nothing more he could do for her, he walked towards the door.

CHAPTER SEVEN

Hopkins called the Earl at his usual time in the early morning.

When he had drawn back the curtains, he spoke up,

"Good morning, my Lord. There be a letter come from the British Embassy for you."

He put it down on the bed beside the Earl and he picked it up.

He recognised at once his secretary's handwriting and wondered what could be so urgent that he had written again.

Mr. Barrett had already written to say that Sadira's horse and her dog had been removed from Langbourne Hall to Kensall Park on his Lordship's explicit instructions. They were both settling down quite happily.

The Earl now opened the letter and the first words he read made him stiffen.

Mr. Barrett had written,

"My Lord,

I am writing to tell you that the newspapers have today announced the death of the Marchioness of Langbourne resulting from a regrettable shooting accident which involved Lord Cairn."

The Earl drew in his breath.

He knew Lord Cairn. He was an eccentric old gentleman, who was a member of White's Club.

It amused him when he went out at night to carry a revolver with him in his pocket.

When he was approached by footpads, which was inevitable around Piccadilly, he would draw his revolver and confront them with it.

When they then ran away terrified, he would fire harmlessly into the air or onto the ground after them and this caused them to run even quicker.

He greatly enjoyed what he considered to be 'good sport', although the Earl and the other members of the Club considered it undignified behaviour for a Peer of the Realm.

Mr. Barrett's letter continued,

"Because I thought that your Lordship would want to know the full circumstances, I got in touch with the butler. He told me, of course, in the strictest confidence that the Marquis had gone away for the night, but returned home unexpectedly.

He found her Ladyship and Lord Cairn in compromising circumstances and threatened them with divorce proceedings.

Apparently Lord Cairn sprang out of bed and, seizing his revolver, threatened to shoot his Lordship.

Her Ladyship screamed and in an attempt to avoid a scandal tried to force up Lord Cairn's arm. Unfortunately she also pushed him and, as he had been drinking heavily, he fell backwards. In doing so he pulled the trigger and the bullet buried itself in her Ladyship's breast.

The doctor was sent for, but her Ladyship never regained consciousness and died the following morning. His Lordship is naturally deeply distressed and, if your Lordship has been successful in finding Lady Sadira, perhaps you could then inform her Ladyship of the circumstances.

I remain.

Your obedient servant,

Robert Barrett."

The Earl read the letter through twice.

Then he told himself that, as far as he and Sadira were concerned, nothing could be more fortunate.

He could understand exactly what had happened.

The Marquis, having been outwitted once, was determined not to let it occur again and he knew that Lord Cairn, besides being an eccentric, was also a heavy drinker.

It was easy therefore to see how such an accident could have happened.

While the Earl was dressing, he sent Hopkins to find out if Sadira was awake yet.

When he came back, the valet reported,

"According to the maids who's lookin' after her Ladyship, she's sleepin' like a baby, my Lord. If you asks me, it's the very best thing her Ladyship could do."

"I agree with you," the Earl said. "Tell the maids I am going driving with the Sultan, but they are to insist that her Ladyship stays in bed and rests. She should not attempt to get up today."

"I'll tell 'em, my Lord," Hopkins replied, "but I expect, it's what they'll be thinkin' themselves. They're a lazy lot when your Lordship compares 'em to what English lady's maids do."

The Earl smiled, but did not reply.

When he had finished dressing and had eaten his breakfast, he reckoned that the Sultan would be waiting for him.

*

Sadira stirred in her comfortable and felt as if she was coming back to life through a very long dark tunnel.

She thought that she must have slept all through the night.

When she eventually opened her eyes, she could see that the sunshine was streaming in through the windows of the room.

For a moment she could not think where she could possibly be.

Then she remembered all that had happened last night and how the Earl had saved her in the nick of time from a blazing inferno.

'How can he have come to Fez at all and just at the right moment?' she asked herself.

When she had found the baby in the back room, she had come out just as the staircase had collapsed.

It had spread the fire all over the ground floor and the front wall of the house was a mass of flames.

It seemed to her then that there was nothing that was not on fire and burning out of control.

She had thought that both she and the baby in her arms would be burned to death.

'Help me – *help me* – God!' she had prayed fervently.

At that moment she had seen a tall figure shrouded in a *djellaba* coming resolutely towards her through the flames.

The strange robe he was wearing disguised him, but she knew instinctively who it was.

Her prayer had been answered and there was no need for her to say anything.

She only knew, as he covered her with the wet *djellaba* and picked her up in his arms, that she need no longer be afraid.

She had hidden her face against his shoulder as he had told her to do.

Later, as he carried her along the twisting darkened streets, she had felt herself drifting away.

There was now no fear, only a comforting feeling of safety and thankfulness that she was still alive and she thought now that she must have been hardly conscious.

The Earl had carried her into The Palace and straight up the stairs.

He had set her down on the bed and she had looked up at him.

Then he had bent his head and kissed her.

She could still feel, as she thought about it again and again, the sudden shaft of ecstasy that had run through her.

It was like nothing she had known before in her entire life.

And she told herself now that he had kissed her only as he might have kissed a child.

But there had been nothing childlike in what she had felt.

Although she hardly dared to admit it to herself, she realised that she wanted him to kiss her again.

She lay thinking of the Earl just as a man, not worrying as to why he was here or how he had found her.

She found herself drifting away again into a dream world that made her feel very happy and content.

A short time later a maid peeped in to her bedroom see if she was awake.

Sadira raised her head to ask the time and was told that it was just after midday.

'How can I have slept for so long?' she asked herself incredulously

She knew that it was a combination of the voyage, the long ride from Tangier and the sheer terror of the fire.

The maid brought her some food to eat and a colourful bowel of exotic fruit, which she greatly enjoyed.

When she suggested that she would like to get up, the maid told her in broken French that his Lordship had gone driving with the Sultan.

He had strict her given orders that she was to stay in bed and rest for the day and indeed Sadira had no wish to do anything else.

But she felt guilty at allowing herself to be treated as an invalid when she had promised to help Father Christopher in his good works.

However, there were, she now remembered, a great number of people in the house where she had stayed.

She knew that they would hasten to help him as she had done before.

It grew very hot in the afternoon and Sadira drifted off to sleep again.

When she finally awoke, she was aware with a leap of her heart that she was not alone in the room.

Sitting beside her on the divan was the Earl.

She gave a little cry.

"I have been asleep and I did not know – you were – here."

"I was beginning to think that you were Mrs. Rip Van Winkle!" the Earl teased her.

Sadira sat up in the bed and rested her back against her pillows.

She had no idea how lovely she was looking with her fair hair falling over her shoulders nearly to her waist.

She was wearing a diaphanous nightgown, which she had brought with her because she thought that it was lighter than any of her others.

She did not feel in the slightest self-conscious even though she was in bed and she only thought how handsome the Earl was and how strong and dependable he looked.

"You are all right?" he asked with a note of concern in his voice.

"I am being – lazy only on your – instructions, my Lord," Sadira answered him.

She gave a little laugh as she added,

"Now that I am feeling so well, I want to dance for joy because you – saved me and that – dear little baby."

"How could you do anything so reckless and yet so incredibly courageous?" the Earl asked. "When I saw you running through the door of the house and into the flames, I just could not believe my eyes!"

"How could I – let the baby – die?" Sadira asked. "And how could – you be so – wonderful as to be – there so instantly in answer to – my prayers?"

"I thought you were praying," the Earl commented, "and it was only your prayers that got us safely out of that burning house."

Sadira smiled at him and he said,

"I have a great deal to tell you."

"I am listening and I only hope you are not very – angry with – me."

"I am not angry, but shocked and horrified that you should have run away as you did," the Earl replied. "I understood, of course, why you wanted to do so."

Sadira shyly looked away from him, knowing that he was referring to her stepmother.

"Your reasoning, however," the Earl went on, "was completely wrong."

"Wrong?" Sadira queried.

"You said in your letter that you thought that, when we were together, I was wishing that there was someone else in your place. That, however, was never the case at all."

Sadira could not look at him and he continued,

"You thought I was in love, but in fact I have never in the past been in love. That was why I was so determined not to marry."

Sadira turned to look at him and her eyes were very wide.

"Y-you have – never been in love?" she asked. "I don't – understand."

"Then let me explain it to you," the Earl offered. "You think, because you are young, of love as the ideal and perfect love that we all seek but few are privileged to find."

He saw that Sadira was looking puzzled as he carried on,

"But while a man may seek for what he thinks of as a jewel without fault or the purity of a lily, he would hardly be inhuman if he refused the other flowers that he encountered by the roadside."

"What you are – saying," Sadira said hesitatingly, "is that – you have found other women – attractive – but you did not l-love them."

"That is it exactly," the Earl nodded. "It is quite natural for a man and a woman to be attracted physically to each other. For the man it is a pleasure to make her his and what he feels is of great satisfaction to his body, but not to his mind and soul."

He dropped his voice as he added,

"What I have been seeking all my life is the love that my mother taught me is a part of God. I knew that when I found the woman I really loved I would worship her and hold her in my arms for Eternity."

Sadira felt herself quiver at the note in his voice as he said the last words.

Before she could say anything, the Earl went on gently,

"And that is what I felt last night when I saw you standing with the baby in your arms and the flames threatening to consume you."

"Y-you – *saved me*," Sadira managed to stutter.

"By the mercy of God I saved you," the Earl replied, "but, my darling, it is something you must never do again unless you wish to destroy me."

He saw the sudden radiance that transformed Sadira's face and he reached out his hands to take hers.

He felt her quiver at his touch and he then spoke to her very softly,

"I love you! I love you with my heart and soul and I have been searching the earth and sky for you all my life!"

"It – cannot be – true!" Sadira whispered.

'It is true!" the Earl insisted. "I intend to make you love me as I love you and to make certain that you cannot escape me again."

Sadira felt as if the sunshine dazzled her eyes.

She was bemused, bewildered and at the same time completely entranced by what the Earl was saying to her.

It was impossible to find words to answer him.

His fingers tightened on hers as he said,

"So that you can never escape me, I have arranged that in a very short while Father Christopher will come here to marry us."

"To – marry – us?"

Sadira could hardly breathe the words, but the Earl heard them.

"I am sure you know that a Missionary carries a consecrated stone with him," the Earl said. "It seems that he can administer a Holy Sacrament wherever it is needed. When I related to him what I wanted, he told me that he is very proud of you and would be delighted to conduct our Marriage Service."

"Are you quite – quite certain that – you want to – be married?"

"I am more certain than I have ever been about anything," the Earl declared. "And, as I have already told you, I am taking no chances, I will not allow you to leave this bed until you are my wife!"

Unexpectedly Sadira laughed.

"I know – this is – a dream," she protested. "I ran away from England because I thought it would make you happy never to see me again, but now you are telling me we are – to be – married!"

"We *will* be married," the Earl affirmed, "and I know, my lovely one, we will be very happy. As you said yourself, we have our horses in common."

He saw the question in Sadira's eyes before she asked it.

"Swallow is waiting for you in my stables and Bracken is having a great time with my dogs."

He saw her apprehension fading away and then he said quietly,

"I have some other news for you. Your stepmother is dead."

"Dead? How can – she be – dead?" Sadira asked in astonishment.

"I understand from a letter that my secretary sent me that it was a shooting accident."

Sadira gave a little gasp.

"P-Papa did not – kill her?"

"No, no. It was a man called Lord Cairn, who always carries a revolver with him and also drinks too much."

He paused and then continued,

"I understand that he was showing your father the revolver, but the trigger was faulty. The gun went off and the bullet struck your stepmother."

The Earl guessed as he spoke that this was the story that would appear in the newspapers and it was all that Sadira needed to know.

He had no wish for her to receive another shock by learning the truth of what had actually happened.

But she was more intelligent than he gave her credit for.

"Oh, poor Papa!" Sadira exclaimed. "If he has been deceived again, he must be very upset and angry."

"He is," the Earl replied, "and that is why, my darling Sadira, I think that, after a short honeymoon, we must go back so that you can comfort him."

Sadira felt that it was wrong to be glad that her stepmother was no longer alive, but she could not help feeling that a heavy weight had been lifted from her shoulders.

There was no longer a ghastly fear at the back of her mind, a fear that, if she and the Earl returned to England, the Marchioness would somehow contrive to make her life a misery.

And she would certainly try everything she could think of to break up their marriage.

Sadira felt now as if the sunshine had suddenly become more dazzling and she could hear angels singing.

The Earl was watching closely the expression on her face.

"I think," Sadira said softly, "that what I am feeling is – love and it is – very – very wonderful."

"I will teach you to be sure that what we feel for each other is the perfect love that we both believe in," the Earl answered.

He put his arm protectively around her shoulders.

Then he was kissing her, at first very gently and then, as he could feel the softness and sweetness of her lips, more possessively.

He kissed her until Sadira felt that the ecstasy was beyond anything she had imagined or dreamt love would be like.

It was perfect, incredible, sublime!

When the Earl moved, she held onto him as if she was afraid that he would leave her.

"I love – you," she whispered, "I do – love you! Please – go on – loving me."

"You may be quite certain of that," the Earl assured her.

Then he was kissing her again.

*

Later there was a sound outside the door and the Earl was aware that time was passing by rapidly.

He looked down for a moment at Sadira's face and he thought that it would be quite impossible for anyone to look more beautiful or more spiritual.

It was that, he knew, which had made her, from the very beginning, seem different from all the other women he had known.

Now he recognised that the glorious sensations they had aroused in him were as nothing compared with the rapture that he felt in his whole body when he kissed Sadira.

He rose from the divan and walked towards the door.

Outside he saw great clusters of flowers and he thought that the Sultan's maids were waiting to bring them into the bedroom.

He reckoned that by now Father Christopher would be arriving and, leaving Sadira to the maids, he went to find him.

When the Earl reached the hall, Father Christopher was just stepping out of the carriage that had been sent for him by the Sultan.

Hopkins was there as well and the Earl saw that he was holding in his hand a large bouquet of Madonna lilies.

He had ordered him to buy them for Sadira from the flower sellers in the Old City.

He knew in his heart that to him she would always possess the purity and perfection of a lily and this again was a superb enchantment that he had never found in any other woman.

Hopkins took Father Christopher to a room where he could put on his surplice and then the

Earl went into Sadira's room to see if she was ready.

When he walked into the bedroom, the maids all covered their faces and faded away.

The Earl stood at the foot of the divan and looked down at his bride.

He had remembered to order a wreath fashioned of tiny white flowers and now it was on her head.

To him it was more becoming than any diamond tiara could possibly have been.

He put the lilies on the bed in front of her and, as she smiled at him a little shyly, he realised that he was indeed the luckiest man in the world.

He was prepared to challenge anyone who contradicted him.

"Thank – you for the lovely – flowers," Sadira murmured.

They scented the room and were massed on either side of the bed and it appeared as if Sadira was in a bower of roses, orchids and camellias.

There were no words, the Earl thought, to express how lovely she looked.

Then the door behind him opened and Father Christopher came in.

He was wearing a white surplice and in one hand he carried his consecrated stone and in the other he held a Prayer Book.

He put the stone down on the table beside the bed.

Then, opening his Prayer Book, he solemnly began the Marriage Service.

It was a short one, but very moving.

When the Earl placed the gold ring on Sadira's finger, she could hear the angels singing once again.

She felt too that her mother was near her, approving of her marriage and wishing her all the happiness in the world.

When it came to the Blessing, the Earl knelt and Sadira put her hands together in the age-old gesture of prayer.

She was absolutely sure, as Father Christopher made the sign of the cross and blessed them, that they would be happy for ever.

Their love would deepen as the years passed by because it was the love that came from God.

Then, without speaking, Father Christopher left the room.

The Earl put his arms around Sadira.

"My darling, my wife!" he sighed. "Now you are mine and I will never ever lose you."

"And I will never – leave you, my wonderful – husband," Sadira whispered. "I feel – our marriage has – united us so closely that we are – now one person."

"That is exactly what we shall be for always," the Earl promised.

Then there were no words to express what he was feeling in his heart and soul.

He kissed her until the room swung dizzily round them and they were flying into the sunlit sky.

A little later Father Christopher came back.

"Before I leave, my Lady," he said to Sadira, "I want to tell you that your bravery in saving the little baby last night has been of immense benefit to me and to all the Christians in Fez."

Sadira looked surprised and he explained,

"The child is a Muslim and, because you saved him from certain death, the Muslims have asked me to express their gratitude to you."

He paused and then continued,

"What is more, they have promised to stop their persecution of the Christians in Fez and to try to live beside them amicably."

"I am so glad, Father, so *very* glad!" Sadira enthused.

"And so am I, my daughter. At the same time I am sorry to lose my disciple."

"We shall always take an interest in what you are doing, Father," the Earl promised, "and we will come back to see you next year, if you will still be working here."

"I would like that," Father Christopher said simply, "and I must thank you again, my Lord, for your very generous donation towards my cause."

Sadira looked at the Earl and smiled.

It was so like him, she thought, to help Father Christopher.

"Now I am leaving you," Father Christopher said, "but I hope that I shall see you again before you leave Morocco."

"That may not be possible," the Earl replied. "Sadira has to go home to her father, so we are having only a short honeymoon before we return in my yacht, which is anchored at Rabat."

"The Sultan has told me that he has lent you his Palace by the sea," Father Christopher said. "It is a very beautiful place that might have been made by God for honeymooners."

The Earl walked with Father Christopher towards the door and, when he was moving away down the passage, he went back to Sadira.

He stood for a moment just gazing at her.

Then, when she held out her arms, he threw himself down on the bed beside her.

"I love you! I love you! *I love you*!" he repeated. "So much that I am afraid you will grow tired of me telling you so."

"Only if you – get tired of me saying the same thing," Sadira murmured. "Oh, Norwin, how can – this have happened? I was so – miserable and –

distraught before I left England, and yet now I have – found the Paradise I have longed for here – in the most unlikely place on earth."

"You will find, my darling, that anywhere is Paradise as long as we are together," the Earl replied, "and that is what I will make it for you."

Then he was kissing her, kissing her so that there was no further need for words.

Sadira knew then that they had both found the perfection of love.

It was an inexpressible rapture.

A love that was so totally different from the kind that had shocked and upset her.

And she knew that it was something that would never trouble them again in their lives.

*

Very much later after she had touched the peaks of ecstasy, she realised that she could see the stars shining through the window.

They covered the whole sky like sparkling jewels.

'We have both found the flawless stone we longed for,' she thought.

Then she remembered that it was the stars that had told her to run away and escape.

'Thank you, *thank you!*' she said to them all in her heart.

Then the Earl's arms were round her and he drew her closer to him.

His lips held hers captive and her body, heart and soul quivered with the wonder of his touch.

It was just impossible to think of anything – except for him.

OTHER BOOKS IN THIS SERIES

The Barbara Cartland Eternal Collection is the unique opportunity to collect all five hundred of the timeless beautiful romantic novels written by the world's most celebrated and enduring romantic author.

Named the Eternal Collection because Barbara's inspiring stories of pure love, just the same as love itself, the books will be published on the internet at the rate of four titles per month until all five hundred are available.

The Eternal Collection, classic pure romance available worldwide for all time.

www.ingramcontent.com/pod-product-compliance
Lightning Source LLC
Chambersburg PA
CBHW022105170626
46808CB00002B/616